THE DOOR BETWEEN WORLDS

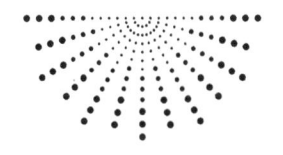

KATHRYN WELLS

Copyright (C) 2018 Kathryn Wells

Layout design and Copyright (C) 2021 by Next Chapter

Published 2021 by Peculiar Possum – A Next Chapter Imprint

Cover art by Cover Mint

This book is a work of fiction. Names, characters, places, and incidents are the product of the author's imagination or are used fictitiously. Any resemblance to actual events, locales, or persons, living or dead, is purely coincidental.

All rights reserved. No part of this book may be reproduced or transmitted in any form or by any means, electronic or mechanical, including photocopying, recording, or by any information storage and retrieval system, without the author's permission.

Through stories, doorways will open that you never knew existed.

PART I
MICHAEL

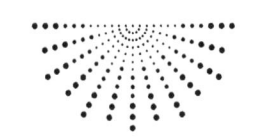

1
GHOST SPHERES

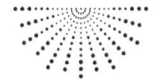

Michael launched himself through the library's sturdy double doors, narrowly missing a well-aimed apple thrown by one of the boys in the year above him. The apple's juice splattered over the tiled floor as it made contact, but at least Michael's uniform had escaped the mess for once.

Mr Rogers, the school librarian, looked up from his desk as the doors banged shut, pen poised over the enormous catalogue that contained the details of every book the library held. He examined Michael critically, taking in the boy's hurried breath and crumpled appearance, and shook his greying head. 'So, you're back again,' he said.

The old man had a short, stubbed nose that looked almost clownish against his serious eyes, and always wore a kilt, despite not being even remotely Scottish, as far as Michael knew.

It was Mr Rogers's job to make sure that every book was neatly in place at all times, unless it was being borrowed or read – a job he took very seriously. If a book stood out even an inch from the others, then Mr Rogers would rush over and put it back in position, as though he feared something might happen to him if he left it.

Michael sighed and made an attempt to straighten his shirt. 'You know this is the only place where I'm safe from them at breaktime, and anyway, this is the only place I *want* to be.' He eyed the bookshelves around him, paying particular attention to his favourite section: fantasy. It was to the right of Mr Rogers's desk and most of the books resembled giant slabs of paper that would take the majority of people a year to read. 'Have you got any new books in about magic yet?' he asked.

'No, the one you returned last time is the newest one we've got. What happened to the book you told me you got for your birthday yesterday? Don't tell me you've finished it already?'

Michael looked away. 'I *might* have stayed up all night reading it,' he said quietly. 'You won't tell Miss Rowan, will you? She'll speak to my mum for sure, and then I'll never be able to read in bed again!'

Mr Rogers laughed. 'No, I won't tell Miss Rowan. Besides, I've spent many a night reading too...though that might be why I have so many wrinkles creeping up on me.' He looked wistfully off into the distance, giving the impression of remembering his younger days. Michael coughed, and Mr Rogers gave a slight start. 'Oh, yes, where were we? Books. Now, I *have* got a new one in about the Greek myths. Are you familiar with them?' he asked, gazing at the shelf behind him and pulling out a book still wrapped in cellophane.

'A little bit, but I've never actually read any,' Michael said. 'They're about the gods who live on Mount Olympus, aren't they?'

'Most of them, but not all,' Mr Rogers said. 'Actually, my favourite is the tale of Medusa.'

'Medusa? Isn't she the one with snakes for hair?'

'Indeed she is; I thought you might recognise her name. It is one of the more well-known myths, after all. There are lots more in the book, some that even I haven't heard of before. Feel like giving it a try?'

Michael eyed the book hungrily. His interest was always stirred when he found a book that contained stories that most people had never heard of. Mr Rogers grinned at him, revealing two very crooked front teeth, and without waiting for an answer, unwrapped the cellophane around the book. He stamped it with the date he wanted it returned by, and then dropped it into Michael's eager hands.

Michael could smell the pages, the crisp scent of paper and freshly printed ink that only came from new books. 'Thank you, Mr Rogers,' he said, clutching it to his body and running off to find his favourite corner of the library where he could read uninterrupted until the end of break.

He opened the cover, turning the pages until he reached the chapter list. The one about Medusa was halfway through, but as Mr Rogers had said it was his favourite (and as he usually had good judgement regarding these things), Michael turned straight to it.

Medusa was a creature called a Gorgon, with the torso and face of a woman, but the tail of a snake. She had a gaze that could turn any living thing into stone if you looked her in the eyes, and her hair was made up of live snakes.

Instantly, Michael found that he was being drawn into the story, turning page after page, reading about all the people who had tried to challenge her and had been turned to stone, quite forgetting that the bell was about to ring.

When it did, he jumped violently, almost losing his place. Quickly, he took a bookmark out of his pocket and marked his page, before making his way back to the classroom where Miss Rowan was waiting.

Instead of smiling at him like she usually did, her brow creased and a frown twitched at the corners of her mouth. But that wasn't all that was strange. The polka dots on her dress were moving around, floating and rippling across the material. No one else seemed to have noticed. Then Michael realised that the dress had been plain earlier that morning, and the truth about what he was seeing began to sink in.

Not good. Trying to hide his concern, he took his seat at the back of the class, watching the polka dots dart around, getting bigger by the moment. They weren't actually dots, they were ghost spheres –

balls of ghostly matter that, for some reason, only he could ever see. They were attracted to people in bad moods, and apparently Miss Rowan was in a *very* bad mood.

'It seems,' she said, speaking slowly and fixing her gaze firmly on Michael, 'that some of you didn't take your work on writing about what you would like to be in the future seriously. I would like to remind you all that things like wizards, spells and magical creatures *do not exist*, and that pretending they are real is what only the infant classes do.'

A sinking feeling hit his stomach. Although she was addressing the whole class, he knew her words were directed solely at him. For some stupid reason, he had been compelled to write about his ambition to train as a wizard. He knew that to everyone else, the idea would seem ridiculous, but he'd believed that wizards existed ever since he was a toddler. And after reading the book his father had given him for his birthday, it had only served to convince him further.

On the outside, the book looked like any other, but the details inside were so well written that it sounded like the author had actually been there. The story was simple; a wizard named Ramble, the most powerful in the Kingdom of Treeshallow, had been enlisted by the king to battle a horde of demons known as the Desrai. What was puzzling about it, though, was that Michael seemed to know things that hadn't even been written down. Like the king's daughter, who was only mentioned once because she had been taken somewhere safe away from the battle. Michael knew there was more to her tale, he *knew* that Ramble had once cured her of a terrible illness that had swept the town, and that her mother had contracted it too, but the disease had progressed too much for Ramble to save her.

Michael had searched the entire book afterwards, trying to find some trace of it; there simply wasn't one. Yet he was sure it had happened, just as he was sure his mother had been angry at his father that morning for falling asleep at his desk instead of sorting through the bills.

As Michael shook his mind back to reality, he noticed that Miss

Rowan was now standing an inch from his desk. The ghost spheres were even bigger now, and were trying to merge into one. '*Go away,*' he told them, hoping that it would work. He'd done it twice before, but there had only been one or two then, not a whole swarm.

The ghost spheres resisted, and now everyone was staring at him. Miss Rowan looked furious.

'I *beg* your pardon?' she said, her voice cracking.

'I'm sorry, Miss Rowan. I wasn't talking to you. I was talking to...' he faltered, unsure of what to say.

'Talking to who? Some magical creature that only you can see? A unicorn, maybe, or perhaps a dragon?'

'No, they're ghost spheres,' he uttered before he could stop himself. Why had he said that? There were times when telling the truth was necessary, he knew, but this really wasn't one of them.

Miss Rowan sneered, and the classroom erupted in laughter. It was too much for him. He jumped up as tears clogged his eyes, warping his vision so that her hair looked like snakes as hideous as Medusa's, and ran from the room.

He wasn't headed for anywhere in particular, just somewhere to get away, but his feet took him straight to the library. Crashing through the double doors once again, he swept behind the nearest bookshelf and fell to his knees.

'Michael?' Mr Rogers said, peering around the corner at him. 'What's the matter? Why are you here during lesson time?'

Michael wiped his eyes on his sleeve and looked up at him. 'I...I can't tell you. You wouldn't believe me,' he replied with a sniff.

'Oh, I'm very open minded. Why don't you try me?' Mr Rogers said, helping Michael to his feet. He took him over to the desk and pulled out another chair for Michael to sit down in, and found a tin of biscuits in one of the drawers, flourishing it around until Michael reluctantly took one.

As though the biscuit had contained a truth serum, the whole story came spilling out of his mouth before he even had time to swallow. His ability to see the ghost spheres, the story about Wizard

Ramble and how he knew things about it he couldn't explain, Miss Rowan berating him for believing that wizards were real, and even his own dream to become one.

Mr Rogers listened silently, and then took a biscuit for himself. 'Well, I can tell you one thing. Wizards *are* real,' he said, brushing crumbs off his kilt. Michael blinked at him.

'Unfortunately,' he continued, 'Miss Rowan is one of those people who I tend to call "practical minded". Magic is too difficult an idea for her to understand, and if, like you say, she's currently possessed by these ghost spheres, there's no wonder she doesn't believe you.'

'What's so difficult about it?' Michael asked.

'She's a person who needs explanations as to how things work, and given that most people have the idea that magic simply...happens, with no hard or fast rules...she just can't accept it. I know, both you and I are aware that magic has many rules and takes a lot of skill to use, but she doesn't realise that,' Mr Rogers replied.

'You seem to know an awful lot about it,' Michael commented, narrowing his eyes. 'Why? You're not a wizard, are you?'

Mr Rogers smiled, though his eyes looked sad. 'No, I'm not a wizard. But I did know one once, a long time ago before you were born. I believe *his* name was Ramble, come to think of it.'

'Really? You *knew* him?' Michael said. 'How?'

Just then the library doors banged open, revealing Miss Rowan. Her expression emitted pure rage, and the ghost spheres on her dress had almost formed into one. Mr Rogers frowned, and then said softly, 'I think it's time for you to leave.'

At first Michael thought Mr Rogers was talking to him, but then he followed his gaze and saw that the ghost spheres were disappearing. As the last one vanished, Miss Rowan shook herself.

'Whatever am I doing in the library?' she said, and then caught sight of Michael and Mr Rogers. 'Mr Rogers, you should know better than to allow a student in here during class time.'

'I do apologise, Miss Rowan,' he replied mildly. 'I've discovered that we have woodworm on one of the bookcases over there. Michael was helping me move the books somewhere else.'

She arched an eyebrow, then gave them a warm smile. 'I suppose I can allow that,' she said finally. 'But make it quick.' With that, she waltzed out of the library, the usual lightness back in her step.

2
THE NOTE

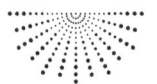

As soon as the sound of Miss Rowan's heels had disappeared down the corridor, Michael turned to Mr Rogers. 'Why didn't you tell me that you could see them too?'

'See what? The woodworm?' Mr Rogers asked, looking intently at the bookshelf as though it really did have them.

'No, the ghost spheres. You must be able to see them, because you told them to leave and they did.'

'Oh, those. Well, until today, I didn't know that you could see them, either,' he said, now going over to the bookshelf and sorting out a trilogy that someone had placed in the incorrect order.

'But that's because I didn't think anyone would believe me,' Michael explained.

'Exactly. I can't very well go around telling just anybody; they'd say I was crazy. If I had known that you could see them, I would have told you. But I didn't, so that's that,' Mr Rogers replied, returning to his desk and sitting behind it.

'But how did you manage to get rid of them so quickly? When I tried, they wouldn't even budge,' Michael said, shifting in his chair.

'When there are as many ghost spheres as that, then you must keep your mind very calm and clear. You have to think of nothing except banishing them.'

'And that's the key to it?'

'More or less. Though it does help to have more experience, I admit. I doubt that I'd have been able to do it at your age. And that was at a time when they were much more frequent,' Mr Rogers said, but then added, almost to himself, 'Yet they do seem to be on the rise again.'

He realised that Michael was staring at him and coughed, slightly embarrassed. 'Anyway, that should be enough time to convince Miss Rowan that we've been moving books. You'd better get back to class.'

Michael stood up, but then remembered that Mr Rogers had known Ramble. That the wizard really was real. 'Can you introduce me? To Ramble, I mean?'

A pained expression crossed the old man's face. 'I'm afraid I've lost track of him over the years. I have no idea where he is,' he said. 'But perhaps you might come across him by yourself one day.'

Miss Rowan didn't say anything to Michael when he got back to class, but she was cheerier in her teaching than she had been for weeks. Usually it took a person days to get back to normal after the ghost spheres lingering around them had been chased away, but she had recovered instantly. Was it really just down to experience and having a clear mind like Mr Rogers said?

As he took his seat at the back of the class and got out his maths book, Michael discovered that something else was bothering him. He thought he would still be stunned that Ramble was real, but the more he considered it, the more it seemed obvious. Hadn't he thought the details in the book were exceptional for a story that wasn't true?

Miss Rowan glanced over, noticing his vacant stare at the wall. Sensing her eyes on him, he started, snapping his pencil lead on the paper. Even if she was back to her usual cheery self, he didn't want to give her any reason to punish him, particularly when his mother always made such a fuss if he was given detention, sometimes banning him from reading for a week.

He stuck his head down and carried on with his work. After a minute, he felt her gaze move to someone else, and let out a small sigh of relieve. Before he could relax, however, she appeared next to him, holding a piece of paper.

'Please make sure you give this to your parents when you get home,' she said, and then added softly, 'I know you like to immerse yourself in stories, Michael. But you must learn how to keep your imagination separate from real life. For your own sake.'

The bell rang, and after hastily packing his things away, he ran out of the door at full speed, without looking back. As soon as he got outside, he spotted his father waiting. Steeling himself, Michael handed over the note. But after a brief scan, his father crumpled it and put it in the nearest bin.

'I don't know what happened, but clearly she has no understanding of how inspiring books can be,' his father said. 'Then again, your mother has never really understood that either,' he added, glancing about as though she might suddenly appear. It made Michael laugh, and as soon as he did, he felt a lot better. His father might not be able to see the ghostly creatures like he could or have a desire to learn magic, but he did know about books. Michael supposed that was where he got his own love for stories from. That, and spending hours during every school holiday helping out in the bookshop that his father owned in town. His mother worked there too, but she dealt with the financial side of things rather than the books themselves. She still enjoyed reading, but for some reason she never got as excited about them as Michael and his father, even if it was a book that they knew was good. His father said it was because she had trouble 'letting herself go', but Michael had never understood what that meant.

Neither of them mentioned the note to his mother when they got back. Instead, they sat down to dinner talking about a new series of books that had arrived at the bookstore. His mother rolled her eyes and smiled as the conversation eventually turned to what the difference was between a wizard and a sorcerer, something that they loved to argue over for hours.

After they had finished, and Michael had been told to go to bed, he slumped down on his mattress in his pyjamas and thought about his conversation with Mr Rogers.

Maybe if Michael asked him at lunch time tomorrow, Mr Rogers would find a way to get in contact with Ramble again so that Michael could meet him. After all, if he really wanted to become a wizard, then there would be no better teacher than him. Ramble was so strong that the demons hadn't even gotten close to the palace, even when the odds had been overwhelmingly against him.

He sighed, thinking about how great it would be to learn magic. Even with a little bit, he would be able to do so much.

'Michael, it's time for sleep,' his father said, knocking on the half open door so as not to disturb him too much. He poked his nose around it and saw Michael with his head in his hands, staring at the floor. 'What's up?'

'It's nothing, dad,' Michael said, sighing again and lying back on his pillows. There was a thump as something dropped off the bed and onto the floor. It was the book Mr Rogers had given him about the Greek myths.

'*Tales of Great Olympus,* huh?' his father read as he examined the cover, before placing the book on Michael's beside table. 'I was fascinated by the Greek myths too when I was your age. Which one are you reading?'

'The one about Medusa,' he said, 'but I've only just started. All I know is that Medusa is one of the three Gorgon sisters, and that her stare can turn people to stone.'

'Ah, well I won't spoil it for you. I think you'll enjoy it. Don't stay up too late, else your mother will tell me off. She reminds me a bit of Medusa sometimes,' his father replied, dropping his voice. 'Don't tell her I said that, though.'

Michael grinned. His mother was strict, but it was usually

because his father got so caught up in the books he was supposed to be shelving that he would forget what he was doing and end up in a muddle.

Saying goodnight, his father winked and closed the door, leaving the bedroom light on. Michael hadn't planned to read that night; the strange events of the day had drained him and made him tired, but now he was curious about the rest of the story. Besides, if it could take his mind off the endless questions about Ramble he had circling around in his head, it would be worth it.

He sat up, punching his pillow into a comfortable position, and picked up the book from the table beside him. Opening it, he found his page and began to read.

The story moved on from Medusa to a young man named Perseus, who was the son of the god Zeus and a human woman called Danae. Zeus ruled over the other gods on a huge mountain known as Olympus, the highest one in Greece. Perseus had never met his father, and, unlike the other sons of gods in the Greek myths – such as Hercules, who had super human strength – Perseus didn't seem to have any powers at all.

As Perseus grew up, he noticed that his mother began to receive attention from King Polydectes, from a land called Seriphos. The king's generous and patient demeanour with her was only an act, as in reality he was a vile and cruel man. It didn't take long for Perseus to realise what King Polydectes was really like, and in an effort to save his mother, he tried to stop them from getting married. However, King Polydectes simply challenged Perseus to a task that he knew he wouldn't survive: to slay Medusa and bring back her head. If he succeeded, then Polydectes vowed to leave his mother alone.

Michael gasped as there was another knock on the door, startled so much that he almost dropped the book on the floor again. He had been so absorbed that he'd forgotten where he was.

'I know you're still awake, Michael,' his mother said outside the room.

Michael let out several large, fake snores. His mother laughed.

'That isn't enough to fool me. Come on, now. I know you were up late last night, and if you do the same again you'll sleep through all of your lessons tomorrow. I doubt Miss Rowan would be very forgiving if that happened.'

Michael pulled a face. He would rather not do anything to upset Miss Rowan again; that would draw the ghost spheres back to her. 'Okay, but let me finish this chapter,' he said, seeing that he only had one more page left before he reached the end.

'Alright, but no more after that. When your father and I come up to bed, I'll be checking.'

He listened to her walk away from the door and go back down the stairs, then he found the torch down by the side of his bed and turned off his main light. He dived under his covers with the book and switched the torch on, having no intention of sleeping until he found out how Perseus would get past Medusa when all she had to do was look at him and he would be turned to stone.

'Michael. Michael, please answer the register. I thought we went over this yesterday,' Miss Rowan said, shaking her head at him in despair.

Michael opened his eyes, realising that he had been dozing at his desk. 'Sorry, Miss Rowan. I didn't sleep very well last night,' he lied.

Her eyes fell to *Tales of Great Olympus*, lying beside his workbook, featuring Medusa's terrible face on the cover. 'I wonder why,' she said dryly. 'Please *try* to stay awake.'

His first lesson went dreadfully slow, and his head was too full of Perseus and Medusa and wondering when to ask Mr Rogers about finding Ramble to concentrate on anything else. In the end, his patience ran out and as soon as the bell rang for break, he dashed from the room and sped to the library.

As he went through the double doors, he stopped dead, his mouth hanging open at the sight before him. The library was a mess. Books were littered across the floor, their spines broken and pages torn out.

Mr Rogers's chair was broken into small pieces, and his desk had been overturned.

Michael walked up to it, noticing that all the drawers had been thrust open, their contents thrown haphazardly on the floor. He bent down to gather them up, but saw that one of the pieces of paper was shining, letting out a cool silver glow like moonlight. It couldn't have been doing that when he first came into the room, else he'd have noticed it immediately. So why was it doing it now? And how?

Then he realised that he already knew the answer: magic.

For a moment, he stood battling with a mix of fear and curiosity at what the contents of the paper might be, but then it flashed brighter and he knew it wanted him to pick it up.

Michael, it read. *As you are reading this, my suspicions must have been true. I'm sure whatever mess you've walked into looks far worse than what really happened. I fear that what I'm about to tell you may make you panic still, but I urge you: do not be alarmed. The Desrai that Ramble fought have been looking for me for many years, and now I believe they've found me. If, as I suspect, they take me prisoner, please find the hidden door behind the bookshelf to the right. Ramble lives behind that door; he is the only one who can help me now. I am sorry, it wasn't my intent to involve you in this so soon.*

Mr Rogers.

Michael's hands trembled as he reread the note, making sure he'd understood it properly. The Desrai had kidnapped Mr Rogers, and now he wanted Michael to go and find Ramble so that the wizard could save him?

He pinched himself hard, hoping that he had drifted off while reading and this was all just a dream. Nothing happened. He panicked. What should he do? Should he go and get Miss Rowan, or one of the other teachers? Surely they could deal with this?

But as Michael looked at the note once again, shining even more brightly in his hands, he knew that he had to be the one to get Ramble. Mr Rogers had left this note specifically for him. If someone else could do it, then he wouldn't have done that.

He scanned the last line. *I am sorry, it wasn't my intent to involve you in this so soon.*

What did Mr Rogers mean by that? Had he been planning to tell Michael all about this later on, when Michael was older or had already met Ramble? With so much information dancing about in his mind, he began to feel dizzy.

Michael shook his head and breathed in slowly. He needed to focus on one task. That was the only way he could keep calm. A hidden door behind the bookshelf to the right. Of course! Where else would a secret door be hidden if not in the fantasy section?

As his mind cleared, the urgency of the situation hit him and a rush of adrenaline coursed through his body, spurring him into action. He rushed over to the bookshelf, looking for a way to move it. It was stacked high with books; only an adult could move it by pulling it away from the wall. There must be another way; Mr Rogers would have known that he was too small to move it by himself.

He thought hard. This was the *fantasy* section. It was *full* of stories about magic doors and secret passages. Sometimes, on bookshelves leading to a hidden passageway, there was a fake book that had to be pulled in order for the bookshelf to swing forward. Maybe the same was true for this bookshelf, although he couldn't see any hinges that would let it do that.

Desperate, he ran his hands over every book on the shelf, even the ones at the very top, which he had to stand on a chair in order to reach. All the books were real. He hadn't even seen a button or lever anywhere that he could pull instead.

What should he do now? Perhaps if he ran to get Miss Rowan, she would move the bookshelf for him. But then he remembered what Mr Rogers had said about her. She was a practical person who simply couldn't grasp the concept of magic. She would never believe him if he told her that Mr Rogers had been kidnapped by demons.

He cried out in frustration, not knowing what to do, and banged his fists against the wall next to him. There was a clicking sound, like rusty cogs starting to move again after being still for a long time, and to his surprise, the bookshelf swung forwards.

Behind it, set deep into the wall, was a red, arched door with a knocker in the shape of a tree. The knocker was shining just as the note had done. Michael took hold of it with trembling hands and knocked once.

As the knock sounded on the door, the whole thing shimmered like a haze of heat. Then it opened. He shut his eyes, blinded by a pure white light. He could see it even through his eyelids, but after a few seconds, it disappeared. A tugging sensation caught him in the chest, and without any chance to resist, he found himself hurtling through the doorway into the bright light.

3
TREESHALLOW

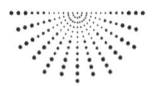

Michael coughed, his mouth full of grass and soil. He spat it out, trying to ignore the sour taste on his tongue, and sat up to look around. Somehow, he had managed to fall face down in a large field, with grass so tall it was up to his knees. He turned around to where he thought the door was, but it had vanished.

A quiver ran through his insides. Did this mean that he couldn't get back?

He stood up, trying to see if there was someone about who he could ask, but even from this level, there was no sign of anyone. He was in an empty field, alone, and he had no idea where to go.

A bird flew over his head, swooping across the sky, and landed in a tree overhanging the field. He gazed at it, taking in the tufted blue tail and the speckled pink and orange feathers that covered its body. It was unlike any bird he had ever seen, even the ones in his father's great encyclopaedia of British wildlife.

Perhaps it was a tropical bird, and the door had transported him to somewhere in the rainforest. The bird cocked his head at him and whistled, and Michael realised that he was wrong. Rainforests didn't have open fields like this; they were dense places full of trees and vines, constantly damp with the moisture from the air. There was nothing like that here.

The bird flew off to his right, and as he followed it with his gaze, he saw that there were small buildings in the distance. He couldn't make them out properly from where he was, but they looked like thatched cottages.

A sign of people! Perhaps one of them knew where Ramble lived and could tell Michael how to get home too. He took one last glance around to make sure that the door definitely wasn't there, and then followed the bird as it soared ahead straight towards the cottages.

It took him a long time to get out of the field, and he spent most of it trying to keep his school shoes out of the muddy puddles that were camouflaged among the tall grass, but after a while he gave up, discovering that his shoes were torn and his toes were poking out. It was like they'd suddenly shrunk. His clothes felt similarly tight and had ripped down the seams in several places, but it was so warm out that it didn't matter.

Now that he thought about it, it was *very* warm, as though it were the height of summer and not the middle of January. Maybe this place was on the other side of the world; he knew there were countries that were now enjoying summer. Was this one of them?

Still, as he watched the bird arc up and down in the sky, flying as though it didn't have any cares, he couldn't shake the feeling that this place might not be in his world at all. It was as though he'd fallen into one of the worlds in the books he'd read; full of strange creatures and, as he came in sight of a particularly large puddle, *hundreds* of ghost spheres.

They were floating there above the watery ground, clumped together like a cloud. They weren't possessing anyone, they were just...there. He had never seen them do that before; at every encounter he'd had with them, they'd always had a host. He jumped around the puddle, fearing that they might latch on to him, but they remained still as though they hadn't even noticed he was there. Uneasily, he sidled away from them, jumping as the bird whistled at him from a tree. It cocked its head again, watching him with beady eyes, as though checking to make sure he was still following.

As he neared the thatched cottages, he saw that there were more of them than he'd originally thought. In fact, it appeared to be a small town, with a stone wall surrounding it, breaking only for the large iron gate in front of him. To the side was a small stone hut, and as he examined it, the bird flew directly towards it, diving straight through the stone. A moment later, the door to the hut crashed open and two men burst, heading straight for him.

They were both dressed in leather kilts with polished metal helmets on their heads, and carried shields and small, sharp swords. He was terrified.

Just he as he was contemplating where to run to, they stopped and cried out in surprise. They lowered their swords and sheathed them quickly, almost embarrassed.

'Wizard Ramble, please forgive us,' one of them said, making a short bow. 'Our messenger told us that someone had come through the Door Between Worlds, and with all the talk about, we naturally assumed it was the demons. We weren't expecting you at all, if truth be told. I'm afraid to say that people were starting to doubt that you'd ever return.'

'Your messenger? You mean that bird?' Michael asked, staring at them both. They were looking back at him with tears in their eyes, as if he were some long-lost relative believed to have been dead. 'And what do you mean by calling me Ramble?'

The man laughed as though Michael had told a joke. 'I see that your years on The Outside haven't altered your humour. But you do look a little strange dressed in those clothes,' he said. 'Where are your robes?'

'I don't have any robes. I'm telling you,' Michael said, 'I'm not Ramble. My name's Michael, and I've come here to *find* Ramble.'

The man laughed again. 'I told you he was funny, Brogar,' he said, turning to the other man, who was identical to him aside from a mole on his nose.

'I'm not trying to be funny. I'm being serious. I'm not Ramble, or any kind of wizard. I can't be, I'm only ten.'

The one named Brogar snorted. 'If you say so, sir, but I've never met a ten-year-old who's so tall. You must be at least six foot. That's almost as big as me.'

Michael looked at him, and realised that he was looking straight *at* him, not *up* at him like he usually did to an adult. He glanced at his body, the truth of why his clothes no longer fit properly finally dawning on him. His hands and arms were much larger, and his legs stretched so far down that for a second, he thought he was on stilts.

He felt dizzy. Seeing a trough next to the stone hut, he rushed over to it and dropped to his knees, peering into the clear water inside. The face that stared back at him was of a full-grown man of at least twenty. It had a short, brown beard covering a pointed chin and curly, close cropped hair, with cool blue eyes that barely resembled his own. It was how he'd imagined Ramble in the book.

'See?' Brogar said, grinning slyly. 'Even if you do pretend to be a ten-year-old, no one will believe you when you're that size.'

'What's happened to me?' Michael cried, scrubbing at his face, sure it must be some sort of illusion. 'Why do I look like an adult?'

Brogar frowned and looked at his friend, who was watching Michael desperately splashing himself with water, trying to make his face go back to normal. 'Are you sure he's joking, Brett?' Brogar whispered to him. 'It seems like he's really confused to me.'

Brett appeared dumbstruck. 'I think you're right. Do you think we should take him to Wilhelmina the Witch?'

Brogar nodded. 'If anyone can help him, it'll be her.'

Without hesitating any longer, they took hold of Michael's arms and steered him through the town's iron gate into a long, twisting lane. It took them past a number of the thatched cottages, made of both wood and stone, and out into a much larger street packed with people. All of them wore medieval-type clothing and carried baskets filled with everything from fruit to rich coloured fabrics, shopping at makeshift stalls to either side of the street where vendors boomed their latest offers to the crowd.

As Brett and Brogar pushed past, a few people noticed Michael dangling between them and let out several gasps. All of a sudden, everyone was rushing forwards to greet him, but when Brogar and Brett explained that he was unwell, they all looked deeply concerned and hurried off, whispering darkly to one another.

Reaching the end of the street, Brett and Brogar made a sharp turn, coming to face a large house decorated exactly like the gingerbread houses Michael's mother sometimes made. It was even embellished with what looked like icing.

As they stepped onto the doorstep, Brogar knocked rapidly on the door, leaving a slight dent in the wood. It opened only a second after he had taken his hand away, revealing a woman slightly older than Miss Rowan. She had dark purple hair that was piled up in a messy bun, more like a bird's nest than an attempt at a hairstyle.

'What is it that you two muscle heads want this time? Can't you see that I'm—'

She stopped as she noticed Michael standing between them, and her mouth formed a large 'o'.

'Wizard Ramble,' she said breathlessly, taking his hand and shaking it just as they had. 'I'm so glad you're back. There are whispers everywhere that the Desrai are active again in Treeshallow.'

'Please,' Michael said. 'I'm not Wizard Ramble. I'm not any sort of Ramble. I'm Michael Sputterson, in year five at Oakhelm Primary School.'

'Oh dear,' the woman said, her face falling. 'Whatever's the matter with him?'

'We don't know, Wilhelmina. That's why we brought him to you,' Brett said.

'I see,' Wilhelmina replied. 'Well, bring him inside and I'll see what I can do.'

She ushered them in and shut the door with a snap so that none of the townspeople could see what was going on. She took them into a large room where the floor sloped down to one side, and a wooden table and chairs stood in the middle. Michael spotted a large cauldron bubbling away in one corner, heated on an open fire.

'Now,' she said, sitting him down on one of the chairs and bringing him a drink of something hot that smelt like roses. 'Drink that and then tell me everything you know.'

Michael eyed it suspiciously, but the smell made him relax so much that he reluctantly swallowed some of it down. It was sweet, but had a bitter aftertaste that was far too similar to medicine for his liking. 'What was that?' he asked, feeling the last bit of tension ebb out of him.

'Something to calm you down. It's made of herbs, nothing more. Now, if you wouldn't mind?' she pressed.

'Oh,' he said, remembering what she'd asked. 'My name is Michael Sputterson, and I live with my parents in a house not far from school. My dad owns a bookshop, and my mum helps him by sorting out all the paperwork and money for it.' Before he could stop himself, he found that he was telling her about the ghost spheres that he could see, and how he could sometimes make them leave when they started making a person too sad. He even told them about how Mr Rogers had chased the ones away from Miss Rowan.

Wilhelmina watched him as he spoke, her eyes tracing every inch of his face, trying to detect any hint of a lie, but when he mentioned that he'd read about Ramble in a book, she let out a sharp hiss.

'This is worse than I thought,' she said to Brett and Brogar. 'You were right to bring him straight to me.' She turned back to Michael. 'Carry on, if you please.'

Michael drank some more of the sweet drink, and said, 'There was something strange about the book; I knew details about the story that weren't even written, but somehow I knew they were true. When Mr Rogers told me that Ramble really was real, I wasn't as shocked as I should have been. It just seemed obvious. Anyway, the next day I went back to ask Mr Rogers if he could introduce me, but he was missing and the library was in a mess. Then I found a note by his desk saying that the Desrai had been after him for years, and now they'd found him. The only way to rescue him was to go through the door behind the bookshelf and find Wizard Ramble. So I did. Well, I was kind of sucked in, actually...'

'And you ended up here, in Treeshallow,' Wilhelmina said. She shook her head and turned to Brogar and Brett, whispering to them. For some reason, it made Michael *very* nervous.

4
MUSHROOM SWEETS

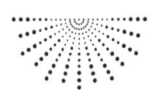

W ILHELMINA TURNED BACK TO MICHAEL. HE SQUIRMED UNDER her penetrating gaze, wondering what was so bad about what he had told her.

After all, it was true. He *had* been pulled through the door and ended up here, growing from a ten-year-old boy to a full-grown man. He still wasn't used to the idea himself, but it was worse with her staring at him like that. It was as though he had some kind of deadly disease.

'Wizard Ramble, I am sorry to say that you've been placed under a spell that not even I, who specialises in reversing spells, can rid you of,' she told him bluntly.

'Well, that would explain why I look like this,' he said, feeling quite relieved that it was something so simple.

'That's not what I mean. Someone has cast a spell on your mind, making you believe that until you walked through the Door Between Worlds, you were this boy named Michael,' she said, shaking her head at him.

'But I *am* a boy named Michael. I don't believe that I am, because

I *really* am. And until Mr Rogers told me that he'd met him, I didn't even know Ramble was real. How could I be someone that I didn't know was real?'

Wilhelmina let out a frustrated sigh. 'Alright, let's pretend that you are this boy, Michael. How do you explain how you opened the Door Between Worlds? Only one person has ever been able to do so, aside from the demons, and that was Wizard Ramble.'

'No one else? Ever?' Michael said, his face falling. 'But it was so easy to get through. All I did was knock, and then...wait, what about the stories I've read about other wizards? I know the characters aren't real, but they must have been inspired by someone. Are you telling me that not even they can get through?'

A small smile touched her lips. 'No, because they all live here in Treeshallow, not in your world. All the stories within The Outside come from dreams that the people have had about Treeshallow.'

He gave her a blank stare. 'What?'

Rolling her eyes, she replied, 'The boundary line between our two worlds is sometimes so thin that events here slip into people's minds as they sleep. The ones who go on to write these dreams down in books believe that they've simply come from their own imagination, but we know better. Tell me, what was the last story you read?'

Michael thought for a moment. 'It was one of the Greek myths, about the Gorgon Medusa,' he said eventually.

Wilhelmina's smile twitched back onto her lips. 'In Treeshallow, we call her Melusa. It's a common thing for names to be interpreted incorrectly on The Outside. Melusa was her true name, and she lived far to the west of here, in the mountains with her three Gorgon sisters. I assume you read about the hero Perolus, who slew her?'

'Do you mean Perseus? I haven't got to that part yet, but I knew he was trying to. Do you mean that he's real, too? And he lives here?' he asked, trying to take in what she was saying.

'He did, but he's been dead for thousands of years. Those myths that you've been reading are very old, you know. And as I said, his name was Perolus. He lived in one of our neighbouring towns when it was just a small village, and mostly spent the rest of his life attempting to convince the fool Ibacus that trying to fly up to the sun using wax wings was a ridiculous idea. I believe that Ibacus is mentioned in the Greek myths of The Outside as well.'

'Ibacus? It sounds familiar, but I think we call him Icarus,' he said, straining his mind back to the other myths he'd heard of. 'So, are you really telling me that every character I've read about lives here somewhere?'

Wilhelmina shook her head. 'Not all of them, no. Some authors do, in fact, make up their own stories from time to time, though I should imagine that most of the well-known characters do live here. I was actually about to suggest that we go and meet someone who I suspect you will recognise.'

Michael raised his eyebrow. 'Who?'

'Oh, you'll see when we get there. He's very skilled at healing magic, as long as you stay away from his mushroom candies. They can have some very odd effects if you're not careful with them.'

She spoke quickly to Brett and Brogar, who had been listening to their conversation with interest. They gave a murmur of agreement and dashed from the room, reappearing a few minutes later with big smiles on their faces.

'The prince said it's fine for you to borrow it. He and Cinderulle are staying at home today, so they don't need it,' Brett said.

Michael narrowed his eyes. Cinderulle sounded oddly like Cinderella to him, and hadn't they also mentioned a prince? Surely fairy tale characters didn't live here too?

'Well, then, Wizard Ramble, it seems our carriage is ready,' Wilhelmina said, taking him by the arm and steering him through the house to the front door. Outside, he saw a large, horseless carriage waiting for them. It was round and orange, with ridges going downwards and a green stalk growing from the top.

'Do you like it?' Wilhelmina said as she opened its door and pushed him inside. He fell awkwardly onto the carved bench, almost hitting the window.

'This is...!' he began.

'The pumpkin carriage,' she said with a hint of amusement. 'I assume you know of it?'

So he'd been right. Cinderulle *was* Cinderella, and this was the carriage she rode to the ball in. He ran his fingers over the interior to see if it was really real. It felt slightly spongy to his touch, but was solid at the same time.

'I've heard that some of the facts were enhanced somewhat by the author,' Wilhelmina continued, without waiting for a reply. 'Apparently they decided it was best for the prince to live in a castle, I believe.'

'Well, yes. Don't princes usually live in castles?' Michael asked, confused.

'Many do, but the prince who lives here is the heir to a farm, not a kingdom, just as his great great grandfather, the prince you know of in the story, was. He and the first Cinderulle lived in a small cottage on the outskirts of town, though I believe it's been sold now.'

'So the Cinderella – I mean, Cinderulle – and the prince that I know are dead, too?' he asked, realising what she was saying.

'Of course they are. The people here in Treeshallow have the same lifespan as those on The Outside. You can't expect the characters you know from older stories to still be alive. Still, the current Cinderulle looks very much like the original, if her portrait is anything to go by, which is quite something considering how distant a relative she is. The prince, however, is a direct descendant and he loves to flaunt that fact.'

'But why? If his grandfather was only the prince of a farm, then there's nothing really special about the story, is there?' Michael pointed out.

A muscle on Wilhelmina's face twitched slightly. 'I think you misunderstand. The farm was, and is, very successful and supplies most of the food in the country. That's an important role in Treeshallow, so the family has been respected for generations. They might not have a castle, or any need of one, but they still have plenty of riches. Compared to how Cinderulle was living with her awful stepmother and her stepsisters, life on a wealthy farm was a welcome relief,' she replied, with a toss of her purple hair. The bun on top of her head rocked precariously, threatening to fall down.

She tapped the front of the carriage with a thin, sparkly stick and it started to roll forwards, picking up speed as it rocked and bounced down the tiny lane.

Michael tensed, alarmed. 'Who's driving? Brogar and Brett went home, didn't they?'

Wilhelmina let out a small laugh. 'I'm driving the carriage,' she said. 'I *am* a witch, after all.' The carriage gave a particularly large jolt as she spoke, and Michael let out a cry. Wilhelmina laughed some more. 'It's such a shame that you're under a spell. I drove you by carriage once before, you know, and if I recall, you thoroughly enjoyed it back then.'

Michael stared at her. His father had always told him that driving was as much an art form as drawing or music, and required great skill if you wanted to do it properly. Wilhelmina's driving was so chaotic that he wondered if skill even came into it at all.

To take his mind off it, he thought back to Wilhelmina's house, considering what she'd said. If there were people here that he knew from stories, then perhaps she was one too. A flash of the gingerbread coloured walls, dashed in icing, and the cauldron boiling on her fire leapt into his mind. He looked at her wide eyed, and breathed, 'Hansel and Gretal!'

'What was that?' she asked, turning to him.

'Your house. It's the gingerbread house from Hansel and Gretal, isn't it?'

'Handle and Petal, I think you mean. Yes, it belonged to my great, great aunt. What of it?'

He whimpered. 'You don't share her...dietary preferences, do you?' he asked slowly.

To his surprise, Wilhelmina chuckled. 'Don't tell me you actually believe that she ate children? Honestly, Wizard Ramble, I know you're confused, but what a ridiculous thing to think! She was well known for chasing people away from her house, though. Liked her privacy, or so my mother once told me, and Handle and Petal *did* pester her a lot.'

After an hour of being thrown around the inside of the carriage, Wilhelmina finally made it pull over by a large clump of mushrooms. At least, that's what Michael assumed they were by their spongy exterior, as they were bigger than any mushrooms he had ever seen, far outsizing most trees.

'Here we are,' she said, opening the carriage door and stepping out, lifting her skirts to do so. Michael climbed out too, glad to be on solid ground again.

'What is this place?' he asked, looking up at the mushrooms and seeing bright, colourful lights darting about under their hoods.

'This is the Mushroom Forest,' she said, following his gaze. 'Those bright lights are fairies. Be careful they don't land on you, they can bite something awful if they don't like you.'

'Fairies bite?' he said, thinking of all the stories he'd read where fairies were lovable magical creatures who simply wanted to help people.

'Oh yes,' she replied, flapping her hand at one as it tried to land on her shawl. 'Come along, I expect he's waiting for us.'

'He who?' Michael said, following her as she strode off further into the forest. 'And how can anyone be expecting us? No one knew we were coming, did they?'

'I see why you were so concerned, Wilhelmina,' a low voice sounded above him. Michael gazed upwards and was greeted with a large cloud of smoke in his face. He coughed, wafting it away with his hand.

An enormous, purple caterpillar was looking down at him from the top of one of the mushrooms, smoking a long pipe.

'Who are you?' Michael asked him curiously.

'No, Wizard Ramble. The question is, who are *you?*' the caterpillar replied, popping a mushroom shaped sweet into his mouth.

5

HOGWASH AND HOKUM

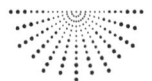

'So you see, that's how I got here,' Michael explained to the caterpillar, after repeating everything he had told Wilhelmina, Brett and Brogar.

'In that case, then perhaps I can help you. Wilhelmina suspects that your condition is a result of you falling foul of a spell, but I have come to my own conclusions,' the caterpillar replied. 'I believe that you, like so many other powerful wizards, had enough of being asked to help with every little matter, and so you escaped to The Outside where you pretended to be this Michael child.'

He inhaled deeply on his pipe and then blew out a large, mushroom shaped smoke cloud that floated straight into Michael's face, making him splutter. 'If that is the case, then I understand completely. I, myself, have often grown tired of people asking for help, and have long dreamt about going to The Outside. However, I hear that caterpillars are small and do not speak there, which I find most uncivilised. As for you, if you wish to keep pretending to be a child, then by all means you may eat one of my mushroom sweets. You should find yourself of a more...shall we say, suitable, size.'

'Now don't go offering him your sweets, Abbleboom,' Wilhelmina broke in sharply. 'You know how dangerous they can be. Why, when you gave them to poor Annie, she shot up and down in size faster than you can say "pop".'

'That was entirely her fault. The girl refused to decide what size she wanted to be,' the caterpillar huffed, exhaling another cloud of smoke. Michael and Wilhelmina coughed.

'You're not talking about Alice from Alice in Wonderland, are you?' Michael said, widening his eyes at the caterpillar. He wondered how it had taken him so long to realise which story he was from.

'Wonderland? Alice? What is this nonsense?' The caterpillar sneered. '*I* was referring to Annie of Treeshallow, who caught her foot in a rabbit hole and hit her head against a tree, making her believe she was in a dream for several years.'

'Alice in Wonderland is probably the name the author on The Outside gave to Annie's story. You know how they always get names mixed up,' Wilhelmina explained.

The caterpillar looked down at Michael and frowned. 'Indeed. An absurd name if I do say so myself. Wonderland. *Wonderland*,' he repeated, shaking his head and popping another mushroom sweet in his mouth. 'How ridiculous.'

'Wait a minute,' Michael said, as he watched the caterpillar eat. 'Why don't the sweets make you change size like they did to Alice – I mean, Annie?'

'I am immune to the ingredients. You, of all people, should know that. After all, you helped me develop them, Wizard Ramble,' the caterpillar replied.

Wilhelmina blew out her cheeks with impatience. 'Are you going to help him, or not?'

'My *dear* Wilhelmina, I have already asked if he wanted to alter his size to appear more childlike. I don't see what else I can do.'

'Oh, bog spatter,' she told him. 'I know you've got more ways of helping people than that. Why don't you use your mind location to find Hogwash and Hokum?'

'Ah, so that is the real reason you came here. It seems that you are getting a little old, Wilhelmina, if you can't even find them yourself,' he said, smiling wickedly at her.

She said a nasty word that made Michael's cheeks turn pale, and the caterpillar chortled. 'I always knew you had a temper. Very well, I shall use my mind location to find them.'

He set his pipe down beside him and touched his forehead with four of his many legs. He closed his eyes and let out a loud, dull hum, which lasted for a number of minutes. Finally, he opened his eyes again and picked up his pipe, drawing deeply on it.

'Well?' Wilhelmina demanded after a long period of silence. 'Where are they?'

'They're at Wizard Ramble's summer house, digging over the vegetable patch,' he replied lazily.

'Thank you,' Wilhelmina said, barely hiding the sourness in her voice.

'Not at all, dear Wilhelmina. I do hope our good wizard starts behaving like himself once he sees them again,' the caterpillar said, waving them away.

Wilhelmina took Michael by the arm again and they left the Mushroom Forest before he even got a chance to say goodbye, getting straight into the pumpkin carriage and driving off, even more unsteadily than when they had arrived. Wilhelmina muttered under her breath and shot dark looks back at the forest until it went out of sight, gradually simmering herself down to silence.

Deciding to be brave, Michael asked her some more questions. 'Excuse me, Wilhelmina,' he began. She turned to look at him as though she had forgotten he was there.

'What is it, Wizard Ramble?' she said, making the carriage jolt around a sharp bend.

Michael steadied himself by holding onto the bench they were sitting on. 'What are Hogwash and Hokum?'

'They're not a *what*, they're a *who*. Hogwash and Hokum are your servants. They've looked after both your summer and winter houses all the while you've been gone. They're Earth Elves. I'm hoping that when you see them, it'll break the spell you're under.'

'So you don't believe what the caterpillar said about me pretending to be ten because I didn't like it here anymore?' Michael asked.

'No, I don't. You would never leave for The Outside to do something like that. Though I have no doubt that you've spent all these years there for some other purpose.'

'How long am I supposed to have been gone, then?' he said, starting to feel unsure about himself.

'About a decade,' she replied. 'I'm sure Hogwash and Hokum can give you a more accurate answer.'

At her words, his throat grew tight, and his hands started to twitch. Ramble had supposedly been on The Outside for the whole time that Michael had been alive. The thought made him feel sick. What if he really *was* Ramble? If so, then was everything he knew about himself a lie?

No. That would mean that his mother and father weren't real, but he knew they were. He couldn't have just made it all up...could he?

'I won't believe it,' he said aloud. 'I'm Michael Sputterson. Not Ramble. My parents are Rick and Rosaline Sputterson, and I'm in year five at Oakhelm Primary School.'

He began chanting it over and over, as though stopping would make it untrue. Wilhelmina looked at him and shook her head sadly, but said nothing.

As afternoon came around, Michael, whose chanting had gradually been replaced with light snores, woke up to see a tall house looming to the right of the path.

He couldn't help but gape when he saw it, for it was truly the most bizarre house he had ever seen. It was shaped like a pyramid, with a chimney poking oddly out of the side near the point. It appeared to be made of brown brick, with some sort of climbing plant covering one of the sides. Several large, round windows looked out onto the path, but there was a silver haze in front of them preventing him from seeing inside.

The carriage stopped outside of it, making him lurch forwards and crash into the pumpkin's inner wall. Wilhelmina, who was unaffected, got out gracefully and held the door open for him. No sooner had he put his feet on the ground, nursing a bruise on his elbow, than they heard a series of excited shrieks from inside the house. The rectangular front door opened with a crash that made the chimney wobble and emit an extra large cloud of smoke, and two small people ran out, one of them leaping up and knocking him to the ground.

'Oh, Ramble! Ramble! We were so worried that you wouldn't return!'

He blinked and stood up, studying them closely. They weren't children, as he'd first thought, but fully grown adults, reaching up to just past his knees. They looked like they'd been shrunk, but they moved around so confidently that he knew they'd always been this size. They both had dark green skin, flecked with gold, and their hair and eyes were a deep brown. He had never seen anything like them before in his life.

The one who'd spoken to him was female; wearing a short dress and soft boots that looked like leather, but on closer inspection appeared to be some sort of tree bark. Her eyes were soft as she looked at him, and she was smiling deeply. The other one, obviously a male due to his stockier build and the stubble on his chin, was dressed in a plain shirt and leggings, wearing boots of the same material as hers. His expression wasn't so welcoming.

'Ten years and you haven't sent us a message even once? You could have died and we wouldn't have been any the wiser,' he said coldly, his voice cracking across them all like a harsh wind.

'Hogwash! That's enough,' the female elf replied, raising her voice. 'I'm sure our master will explain himself once he's settled.'

Hogwash glared at her for a moment, but then shrugged. 'Whatever you say, Hokum,' he said, turning to go back inside.

'So *you're* Hogwash and Hokum?' Michael asked, unable to take his eyes from them.

They frowned at him and looked up at Wilhelmina. 'I suppose you can explain this?' Hogwash asked her quietly.

'Perhaps we ought to go inside and have a spot of tea,' she said. The Earth Elves took her meaning. Hokum gently grasped Michael by the hand and led him inside the strange house, with the other two following along behind them.

As they walked through the door, Michael gasped, wondering if they were really inside after all. They had emerged into a small woodland area, with pine trees and oaks, willow trees and chestnut trees. However, none of them grew past the top of his head.

'Is it normal to have trees inside like this?' he whispered to Wilhelmina.

'No, but this is probably where Hogwash and Hokum sleep. I've never been to either of your houses before, so I don't know.'

'You're right, Witch Wilhelmina,' Hokum said. 'Ramble grew them when he first rescued us. He knew that we would feel uncomfortable sleeping in beds as you humans do.'

'Ramble rescued you?' Michael asked.

'Yes, you did,' she said, unsure if he was joking with her. 'Both I and my brother Hogwash were trapped by the Desrai. We knew our family had escaped and it was too dangerous for them to come and rescue us, so we thought we were done for. But you were walking in the forest that day looking for nettles to make soup, and you saw us and chased the demons away. We've been in your service ever since.'

6

THE TALE OF BEFORE

Hokum led them into what Michael guessed was the living room, filled with plump chairs and footrests all in deep greens and browns. The walls were sky-blue pink, and the carpet was made out of some sort of moss. Altogether, the effect was something like watching a sunset while in the woods.

Somehow, Hogwash had got there ahead of them and was now waiting with a large teapot and four cups, setting them down on a low wooden table as they walked in. Michael saw that as well as cups, there was also a selection of fat, colourful cakes and a jug of milk. He realised he was ravenous.

'Ramble, stop staring at them and eat, will you? That's what you used to do whenever we made cake,' Hogwash said, noticing how Michael was eyeing up the snacks. 'These are just the ones we made in case any guests arrived, so they're only simple. We'll makes some better ones now you're back, assuming our cooking skills haven't gotten too rusty.'

'What do you mean? Surely you've been cooking for yourselves?' Michael asked, after biting into a cake which turned out to be full of some kind of nutty cream and ending up with most of it on his face.

Hogwash might have called them simple, but he thought they were delicious.

Hogwash rolled his eyes and handed him a napkin. Michael took it and wiped his face, sitting down in one of the many chairs. Wilhelmina sat down as well, and Hokum began pouring them both tea.

'You know we don't cook while you're away. There's no point. We live on nuts and berries, not the fancy stuff that you have,' Hogwash explained, looking tired. 'What's wrong with you, anyway? Why did it feel like you were meeting us for the first time?'

'I don't really know,' Michael replied truthfully. After everything he had been told, he was so confused that it felt as though any more information might make him pass out.

'I believe that someone has cast a powerful spell on Wizard Ramble,' Wilhelmina said, straightening up to look important. 'He claims that until he passed through the Door Between Worlds, he has been living on The Outside as a ten-year-old boy named Michael. He has no knowledge of Treeshallow.'

Hogwash gaped at her, but Hokum gave a small cry. 'We feared that this might have happened,' she said slowly, adjusting her simple dress. She exchanged a glance with her brother.

'He's not under a spell, Witch Wilhelmina,' Hogwash said. 'He did it himself.'

'I'm sorry?' Wilhelmina said, putting down her teacup and staring at the Earth Elves. 'Why would he do that?'

Hokum sighed, looking Michael full in the face. 'Our master, Wizard Ramble, grew ill after his battle with the Desrai, though no one knew but us. He told us that he was going to The Outside for a few months, because his illness was one that would ease with rest and, with the news of his victory, he knew that it wouldn't be long until people from all over Treeshallow would come and ask for his help. Rest wouldn't be possible here.'

'We can't know what he did on The Outside for sure,' Hogwash said, taking over, 'but when he didn't come back after some months had passed, we knew that something must have happened. As you know, Wilhelmina, apart from the demons, Ramble is the only one strong enough to pass fully from Treeshallow to The Outside. We couldn't follow him, so we had to stay behind and wait, even if he was in trouble. Given what you've told us, it seems that his illness weakened his body so much that it could no longer handle his magic. If that's true, then he had to find someone to pass it on to.'

He turned seriously to Michael. 'Ramble, when you were the boy, Michael, did you ever believe that magic existed in your world?'

'Yes,' Michael said, startled by the strength of the Earth Elf's gaze. 'I still believe it. All my life I've been able to see the ghost spheres that sometimes possess people, so I thought if things like that are real, then magic must be too. No one else ever saw them though, except for Mr Rogers. He believes in magic too, but I only found that out yesterday.'

The memory of Mr Rogers banishing the ghost spheres from Miss Rowan's dress hung in his mind, and he jumped up, letting out a cry. Mr Rogers! In all the confusion, he had completely forgotten that the old man was being held captive by the demons. 'We've got to help him!' he blurted, as everyone looked at him in alarm.

Wilhelmina rose and took him by the shoulders. 'Wizard Ramble, please calm yourself. Whoever it is that you have to save can wait five more minutes while Hogwash and Hokum explain things, I'm sure.'

'No he can't, the demons have got him,' he said, panicking.

'Do you mean the human they kidnapped from The Outside?' she asked, letting him go.

'He's the librarian from my school,' Michael said. 'The one who wrote the note, telling me about the door behind the bookshelf. The Door Between Worlds.'

Hogwash and Hokum inhaled deeply. 'Please sit down and let us finish explaining,' Hokum said, pulling gently on his sleeve. 'It will only take a few moments more, and if this Mr Rogers is who we think he is, then I'm sure he can hold out until you find him.'

Despite his urge to organise a rescue party, something about the Earth Elf's expression made Michael sit. 'What do you mean, if he's who you think he is?' he asked her suspiciously. 'You know why they captured him, don't you?'

'We can't be certain, but we do know that no human from The Outside knows about the Door Between Worlds,' she said.

'Then how—' Michael began, but Wilhelmina put up her hand to stop him from interrupting. Hokum gave her a look of thanks.

'If Ramble did indeed pass on his magic, then he would have needed to find a new-born child, as a wizard's magic is too strong to be absorbed by a body that is already developed unless the person has received special training. With a child, the magic would be introduced along with other senses, so there would be no danger of their body rejecting it.'

'Wait a minute,' Michael said, before they could shush him. 'My mum did tell me about a strange man she met once, about a month after she'd had me. He asked her if there was anything she wished for, and she said that she wanted my grandfather to live to see my first birthday, I think. He was very ill at the time, and she wasn't sure if he would live that long.'

'Did he?' Hokum pressed.

'Yes, he lived for another two years. If I try hard enough, I can even remember him a little,' Michael said as a vague image of a crinkled face surfaced in his mind.

'Then that was how Ramble transferred his magic to you, by granting your mother her wish. With his powers now part of you, his body would have turned into a normal human's, reaching the age that it actually was. His knowledge of Treeshallow would still remain, as well as his ability to see magical creatures like the ghost spheres, and, if what you say about him banishing them is true, some small remnant of his powers,' Hogwash said. 'We also believe that he would have wanted to watch over you as you grew up. Given that, we think...that this Mr Rogers was Ramble before you, the one that we knew. *That* is why the demons took him.'

'No way!' Michael exclaimed, accidentally squashing the cake in his hand. So *that's* why Mr Rogers had said he'd known Ramble. He used to be him!

'So *this* Wizard Ramble,' Wilhelmina said, nodding to Michael, 'really is just a boy?'

'Yes. Once he stepped through the Door Between Worlds, Ramble's magic stirred within him and gave him the same appearance as the old Ramble. However, it's not only your appearance that's changed, is it?' Hogwash asked, aware of the tears appearing in the corners of Michael's eyes. 'You're finding your memories of The Outside beginning to fade, aren't you?'

Michael wiped his eyes quickly, not wishing anyone else to see. 'I can remember my parents and school, but their faces are all blurry. And the story I read about Wizard Ramble...it feels as though I really lived it.'

'The more time you spend in Treeshallow, the more your memories of The Outside will weaken,' Hokum said softly. 'They won't disappear completely. Your family will always be a part of you, and how you were raised is what makes you an individual, with a different way of thinking than the old Ramble.' She handed him another napkin to wipe the tears now streaming uncontrollably down his face. 'However, his magic is yours now, as is his name, and in time, his memories. In this world, you are no longer the boy Michael. You are truly Wizard Ramble.'

'But what if I don't want to be Ramble?' Michael snapped. 'What if I just want to be Michael, who...who...'

But he stopped. Growing up to be a wizard was precisely what he *had* wanted. He looked at Hogwash and Hokum, who, far from appearing sad, smiled at him.

'You can be just Michael if you return to The Outside,' Hokum said. 'And you may do that at any time. The Door Between Worlds is always open to you, and you can pass from here to there freely. In fact, you have the ability to summon the door anywhere on The Outside; it doesn't have to stay where you found it. You are not trapped in either world.'

'So, I can go home if I want to?' Michael asked, his tears starting to dry on his cheeks.

'Yes, you can,' Hokum said. 'As you're still a boy, your body should return to its normal self as soon as you reach The Outside. If you chose to hide them, no one there would ever know about your powers.'

To his own surprise, Michael laughed. Knowing that he could get back to his family made him feel so happy that rescuing Mr Rogers no longer seemed like such a daunting task. He turned to Wilhelmina. 'So, how do we get to the Desrai?'

7
SMALL, THE DRAGON

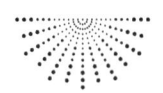

Before Wilhelmina could reply, Hogwash jumped up from his chair, accidentally splashing tea on the floor. 'Come with me,' he said, as Hokum tutted and went to fetch a cloth to wipe it up.

Hogwash took hold of Michael's torn jumper and dragged him out of the room towards a set of wooden stairs. 'Where are we going?' Michael asked, amazed at the strength of the Earth Elf's grip.

'To the observatory,' Hogwash replied, grinning at him and pulling harder, making Michael stumble up the steps.

When they finally reached the top, Hogwash let go and opened the single door awaiting them. The room beyond had sloping, triangular shaped walls that met at a sharp point, and a large fireplace over to one side. Judging by the shape and how long it had taken them to climb the stairs, Michael guessed that they were at the very top of the house, in the tip of the pyramid. 'I thought you said this was an observatory?' he asked, noticing that there were no windows, the room lit instead by four tall candelabras, one in each corner.

'It is,' Hogwash said, watching him. He was holding a long, silver pulley and seemed quite keen that Michael take note of it.

'Then how is anyone supposed to observe anything when you can't see outside?' Michael said. The Earth Elf grinned again.

'Like this.' He tugged on the pulley, and suddenly all the walls swung outwards, as though they were hinged to the floor, revealing the outside. The chimney, however, stayed in place, like a bizarre pillar jutting into the sky. Michael stared at it, wondering how it didn't simply topple over, but then his eyes caught the view beyond it; miles and miles of fields varying from deep green to bright red, with a single road stretching as far as he could see. In the distance, he could make out the town where he'd first arrived, and quite a few more ahead of that. A strong gust of wind crashed against the trees in front of him, blowing off several leaves. Yet the candelabras in the room stayed lit, not even flickering. The air was completely still.

'I don't understand,' he began, but then noticed a faint, bluish mist hanging in the air where the walls had been.

'Nice, isn't it?' Hogwash said, laughing at his expression.

'I've never seen anything like it before,' he replied, extending a finger into the mist. The mist repelled him as if it were solid. 'What is it?'

'It's a barrier against the weather. It was your idea. You wanted to be able to see all the stars without getting cold,' Hogwash said, shrugging. He walked over to the fireplace and tapped it four times.

A coughing sound came from inside it, and a billow of black soot flew up into the Earth Elf's face. Hogwash wiped it away distastefully and tapped again. This time, something dropped out of the chimney and into the ashes still in the grate. It shook itself, making more soot billow about, and strolled out onto the floor.

Michael blinked at it. It was a baby dragon, hardly bigger than his head.

Hogwash picked it up and gave it to him. The dragon looked at Michael curiously and decided to nibble playfully at his fingers.

'Ouch,' Michael said, almost dropping it. The dragon whined and hung its head, making him immediately feel awful. He scratched behind its ears to make up for it. The dragon purred.

'That's Small,' Hogwash said, sweeping up the soot that had now settled on the floor. 'He's our messenger dragon.'

'Where did he come from?' Michael asked, rubbing the dragon's belly as it rolled onto its back in his hand.

'Well, he used to guard a cave up in the mountains that was full of treasure. The previous king asked him to look after it while he was away visiting another Kingdom, but something happened and the dwarves learnt about the treasure and decided to chase him out. They had a hobbit with them, and everyone knows that dragons like to play with hobbits. The dwarves used this to lull Small into a false sense of security, and while he and the hobbit were playing, they managed to trap him outside the cave and took the treasure for themselves. He cried for weeks after that, especially after the king told him off. He didn't know where to go, so you took him in.'

'You mean that Mr Rogers did when he was Ramble?' Michael asked, but Hogwash shook his head.

'No, *you* did. The part that made Mr Rogers into Wizard Ramble is now in you, and soon you should remember everything.'

Michael pulled a face. The more he thought about things, the more confusing they seemed to become. Small yawned in his hands and curled up in a ball, still purring.

'There's a book called The Hobbit on The Outside,' Michael said, changing the subject. 'That had a dragon in it, though he was called Smaug and was a big, terrifying dragon that attacked the dwarves.'

It was Hogwash's turn to pull a face. 'That's the trouble with humans on The Outside. Not only do they always get people's names wrong, but they have to add things that aren't true. Small would never hurt anyone.'

'What about the story I read about Ramble? The author got his name right in that,' Michael said.

'Do you remember the author's name?'

Michael closed his eyes, trying to picture the name that had been on the front cover. 'Samuel Rogers, I think.'

'There you go, then. The previous Wizard Ramble wrote it, and I doubt he would lie about anything that happened,' Hogwash said.

Michael stared at him. Why hadn't he realised that Mr Rogers was the author before?

'Anyway,' Hogwash continued, 'the Desrai never stay in one place for long, so they're very difficult to find. Fortunately for us, dragons have a very keen sense of smell, even as babies.'

'So we can use Small to find out where they are?' Michael asked. Small's purrs had now turned to loud snores, and every so often, a small puff of smoke would come out of his nostrils.

'Theoretically, yes, but Small hasn't flown further than our cabbage patch for years. It'll take him a few days to stretch out his wings enough for such a tough job, so in the meantime, I think we'll have to find the maps you made with the previous locations of the Desrai and work from there,' Hogwash replied.

They heard footsteps coming up the stairs, and Michael turned to see Hokum standing there. Small lazily opened one eye and looked at her, before closing it and promptly going back to sleep.

'There you are,' she said to Michael, shooting a nasty look at Hogwash. 'Before my brother led you away, I was going to ask what you wanted for dinner and whether you would like a bath.'

'Are you sure you don't mind cooking?' Michael said, remembering that she and Hogwash only ate nuts and berries.

'Perfectly sure. Wilhelmina told me that those cakes were the only thing you've had since you got to Treeshallow. You need eat properly; otherwise you won't remember how to use your magic.' She stared at his school uniform, torn and stretched now that he was so tall. 'Perhaps it would be best if we found you some more comfortable clothes, too?'

In the morning, clean and dressed in the long white robes he had read about, Michael got up and went down to the living room. Wilhelmina was already there, dressed in clothes that Hogwash and Hokum had made the previous night while she and Michael had been eating. They were made out of a purple coloured fabric that matched her hair and sparkled whenever she moved.

'I never knew that Earth Elves were so talented at making clothes. It's a shame none of them live near the town. They could make a fortune selling clothes there,' she said as she poured herself a cup of tea from the pot that Hokum had left on the table.

'We're the only Earth Elves that know how,' Hogwash said, entering the room with two steaming bowls of porridge topped with fresh berries. 'Ramble taught us how to make them when we first came to live with him. He used to make his own clothes, you see, but we wanted to help, so he showed us how to cut fabric and use different types of stitch.'

He and Wilhelmina carried on talking while Michael ate his porridge, wondering where Small had gone. During the night, the tiny dragon had slept on his pillow, but when he had woken up, Small had disappeared.

A whining sound came from the kitchen where Hokum was cleaning up, one that only a baby dragon could make. Eating the last spoonful of his porridge, Michael got up and took his bowl out so he could wash it. As he entered the kitchen, he saw her standing on a stool by the sink, with Small lurking beside the stool legs gazing up at her.

He laughed and they both looked at him, surprised. 'I didn't see you there,' she said, as Small ran towards his feet and rubbed against them. 'He always whines like that, trying to get more food. He's already had two helpings of porridge though, and dragons shouldn't really eat anything but meat.'

'Can't you give him some of that instead, then?' Michael asked.

Hokum shook her head. 'We don't have any here, and he refuses to go out and hunt.'

'But didn't you cook us meat for dinner last night?' Michael said.

'No, that was the root of the Bubock plant. It only looks like meat, but really it's a vegetable. Meat is very scarce in Treeshallow, ever since the beanstalk crisis.'

'The what?' he asked her.

'The beanstalk crisis. There was a boy who sold his family's cow for magic beans, which turned into a beanstalk that the Tallmen could climb down. They wrecked a number of villages before the king's army could get them under control. After that, everyone was banned from keeping animals to stop them being traded like that again. The wild animals here are all too magical and strong for humans to hunt, so everyone eats the roots of the Bubock plant instead.'

'Oh,' Michael said, wondering how many more familiar stories he would hear about. 'What about the milk I had yesterday? Where did that come from?'

'That wasn't milk, that was Bubock juice. I'm told it tastes like cow's milk,' she said. 'Here, let me show you.'

She jumped down from her stool and went through a door leading out into the garden. He followed her, and watched as she picked a handful of white berries from a clump of bushy green plants. 'These are Bubocks,' she said, indicating the plants, 'and the juice comes from these berries.'

She gave him one and he bit into it, sucking in the juice. It really did taste like cow's milk. 'That's amazing,' he said, taking another berry from her. 'None of the berries on The Outside taste anything like this.'

'That doesn't surprise me,' she said. 'Bubocks aren't like normal plants; they only grow where there's a high concentration of magic, and according to what everyone says, the only magic on The Outside is whatever spills through from Treeshallow.'

8

THE JOURNEY BEGINS

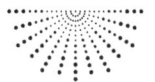

'You're not coming with us?' Michael asked Wilhelmina as she packed her old clothes into the pumpkin carriage, ready to leave.

It was late afternoon, and after several hours of discussion and Hogwash's discovery of a large bundle of maps hidden in the observatory, they had finally come up with a plan to find the Desrai.

According to the most recent map that Ramble had sketched before he'd left for The Outside, the remnants of the Desrai were lying low in the mountains. They were the same mountains Wilhelmina had told him about, the ones where Medusa – no, Melusa, she was called in this world – had lived before she was killed. Her two Gorgon sisters were thought to have perished not long afterwards, in a fight over Melusa's possessions, so the mountains had been uninhabited. Hogwash speculated that this was why the Desrai had settled there after their defeat, for there were no other monsters to chase them out.

However, ten years had passed since then, and though no one wanted to say it, they all knew that the demons could be anywhere by now. Michael thought about how easily they had captured Mr Rogers and wondered if they were lurking somewhere near the Door Between Worlds, but Hogwash said it was unlikely because the people in the town had a direct view there. A horde of demons wouldn't simply go unnoticed.

He and Hokum both theorised that the demons were hiding somewhere not easily reachable, where they would be left alone to build up their ranks.

As they had examined the other maps, some showing the demons in the swamps to the east, or by the coast to the south, Michael had to agree that they might be right. The swamps and the rocky coast were as hard to reach as the mountains. The one difference was that there were many towns surrounding them, whereas not even a single hermit lived near the mountains.

Whichever path they chose, there was no way of knowing whether it was right until Small was able to fly overhead and see. But that would take him a week or more, if Hogwash's memory was right, and Michael couldn't just sit and do nothing. Not when people could be in danger. If the Desrai really had been building up their ranks, then they could have any number of warriors by now. The Royal City might come under attack at any time, and the king wouldn't be able to do anything to defend it. Michael couldn't let that happen, so, as the most likely place for the demons to be, they'd decided to set off for the mountains.

'I would like to go with you, but I'm afraid battling demons is beyond my powers. Besides, I have to return the carriage to the prince and Cinderulle. They only let me borrow it for a day, so I'm overdue on returning it as it is,' Wilhelmina replied.

'But what if it's beyond my powers, too? I don't have any idea how to defeat the demons by myself,' he said. 'I can't even use any magic yet.'

She turned to him and put a hand on his shoulder. 'If Hogwash and Hokum are right about you, then both your memories and your powers should return soon. Trust in yourself, and you'll find a way. You're the greatest wizard in all of Treeshallow, after all.'

'I don't feel like I am,' he mumbled miserably.

She sighed. 'If you really do need my help, then there is a spell that you can use to contact me. It's one of the only ones that wizards and witches can both use, because our magic is usually quite different. All you have to do is touch your forehead and say "Contact Locate" while picturing me in your mind. It should allow us to talk to each other telepathically.'

'Telepathically? You mean, just using our minds?' he said. The idea made him choke slightly.

'That's right,' she replied. 'Now, I really must get going. You should too, if you want to make any sort of progress before nightfall.'

Michael thanked her and watched as she climbed into the pumpkin carriage. She waved goodbye to them from the window and then drove away, the carriage rocking precariously from side to side as it went.

'I hope I can do this,' Michael muttered to himself.

Small, who had been sitting on his shoulder, decided to rub his scaly head against Michael's neck. Michael patted him and went back into the house, climbing the stairs to the observatory. The maps were still lying open on the floor, held down with crystal paperweights. He bent down to examine them once more before carefully rolling them up, ready to be packed with the rest of their luggage.

'The carriage is ready, Wizard Ramble,' Hokum said quietly by the stairs. She had been so silent entering the room that he jumped violently, making Small fall off his shoulder and onto the floor. The dragon grumbled and unfolded his tiny wings, giving them a small shake before folding them back against his sides.

'Thanks,' Michael said, gathering up the maps in a big bundle. He looked down at Small and grinned. 'I hope you're ready to start flying again.'

The dragon snorted a small flame at his feet and ran away down the stairs, almost knocking Hokum over. 'I see he's as lively as ever,' she said with a smile. 'He's glad you're back, you know. Hogwash and

I couldn't get him to wake up most days, but this morning he was up well before us.'

She led Michael down the stairs, telling him how the little dragon used to block the chimney up for weeks, and how when he did emerge, the whole room would be covered in soot.

They came to the hallway and she disappeared into Ramble's room for a moment, before coming out with a large suitcase. It was so big that it towered over her and she had to drag it out of the door. 'Let me do that,' Michael said when he saw her trying to pick it up. 'I might as well be useful now that I'm fully grown.'

Tucking the maps under one arm, he picked up the suitcase. The weight of it nearly made him drop it again, but he saw her watching and smiled, hoping the strain wouldn't show on his face.

She laughed at him openly.

'What's the matter?' he asked as they walked back to the front door and out into the garden where Hogwash was waiting with the carriage. Compared to the pumpkin, it was rather ordinary, painted in black with silver accents around the doors and windows.

'It's just that you're starting to act like your old self again,' she said, the gold flecks on her green skin reflecting the morning light.

'You mean, Wizard Ramble was like me?' he said, surprised.

She laughed at him again. 'You *are* Wizard Ramble. Of course you're like you.'

He scowled. 'You know what I mean. I was talking about the old Wizard Ramble.'

This time she didn't laugh, a crease forming on her brow instead. 'I guess you really don't understand yet. But then, I suppose it is complicated for a ten-year-old.' She took a deep breath, and he knew she was trying to think of a way to explain things a bit easier. 'When Wizard Ramble gave you his powers, it wasn't simply his magic that he transferred. It was also the part of him that *made* him Wizard Ramble. All the things he did in Treeshallow, everyone he knew, the way he acted because of it...all of it went to you. Samuel Rogers is what was left. Why do you think he sent you here? It wasn't to *find*

Wizard Ramble, it was for your powers to awaken so that you would *become* him.'

Michael stopped, trying to let what she'd said sink in. So Mr Rogers had been aware that he'd turn into Ramble as soon as he stepped through the Door Between Worlds? Suddenly, the last part of the note Mr Rogers had left him made sense. *I am sorry, it wasn't my intent to involve you in this so soon.* He must have wanted to tell Michael about his powers and about Treeshallow all along, but instead of being able to wait for the right time, Mr Rogers had been forced to send him to Treeshallow much earlier.

'He really wasn't lying when he said he wasn't a wizard,' Michael said, finally convinced.

'No, he wasn't lying. He's not a wizard, because you are,' she said. 'It'll become clearer in a few days. Places and people will start looking familiar without you realising it, and your staff will respond to you again.'

'My staff?' He felt inside his white robes and pulled out a small stick that looked so ordinary he might have simply picked it up off the ground. 'I remember from the story...or is it a memory, I can't tell anymore...this stick transforms into a magic staff, doesn't it?'

'That's right,' Hokum said. 'Once it recognises you, it will transform and your magic will awaken. In the meantime, I believe that you can still try small things without it.'

'Like what?' he asked curiously.

'Like waking up the unicorns.'

She pointed at the carriage behind him, where two large statues were harnessed to it. Michael blinked, wondering how he hadn't noticed them earlier. Each one was shaped like a large horse, except that they each had a single spiral horn growing out of their foreheads.

'What do you mean, waking them up? They're made of stone,' he said, running his hand over their rigid surface to make sure.

'This is how unicorns hibernate. They turn to stone for the winter. Usually they wake up themselves in summer, but these two have always been a bit lazy,' she said, patting one on the leg. 'If you touch their noses and say "breathe", then they should start to wake up.'

Michael looked at the Earth Elf doubtfully but did as she said. He touched the unicorns' noses, hoping that she wasn't playing a joke on him, and said, 'Breathe.'

Instantly, the stone grew warm and soft. Then it started changing colour, from dull grey to vibrant silver. He felt warm breath against his chest and saw both their torsos expand and contract, taking in deep swells of air. Finally, the horns on their heads glowed pale blue, and the unicorns opened their eyes to look at him.

Each of them whinnied and nudged him affectionately, and he rubbed their necks, making them nudge him even more. 'It worked!' he exclaimed, astonished.

'Their names are Lightfoot and Swiftwind. They're the fastest unicorns in all of Treeshallow...when they're awake,' Hogwash said, shooting the unicorns an amused look. They snorted at him and looked away. He laughed. 'Now, are you certain about heading up to the mountains?'

Michael glanced at him and chewed his lip before taking a deep breath. 'I think so. Even if the Desrai aren't there anymore, they might have left traces of where they went,' he said, his voice sounding more decisive than he felt.

'Good,' Hogwash said, and opened the carriage door so that Michael and Hokum could get in. Small, who had been resting on top of the carriage, let out a low yawn and stood up, flapping his wings. He cocked his head at Michael, and then jumped off the carriage and flew into the air. It looked like it took him a lot of effort to stay airborne, but he managed it nonetheless.

'Well, if Small's ready, then I suppose I am,' Michael said to himself, and got in the carriage with Hokum, while Hogwash took the reins and led the unicorns off onto the single road that cut through all of Treeshallow.

9

CROSSROADS

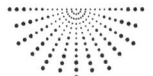

Michael watched Small zooming about in the sky from the carriage window. It was the third time that the little dragon had tried flying that day, and each time, he had managed to keep it up for longer.

At first, he could only stay in the air for about ten minutes, but this time he'd been flying for almost half an hour. He did one last loop the loop before speeding through the open carriage window and onto Michael's lap.

'You're getting much better,' Michael told him, stroking his scaly neck. 'I bet that soon you'll be able to fly for most of the day without getting tired at all.'

'He used to do that all the time,' Hokum said, reaching out her small, delicate hand and scratching behind the dragon's ears. Small purred at her, and left Michael's lap to sit on her's instead.

As she spoke, Michael had a sudden vision of Small flying in the sky, though his wings were much bigger than they were now, and his body was longer, too. 'Hokum,' he asked her, 'Did Small used to be bigger than this?'

She raised an eyebrow at him, smiling. 'Yes, he used to be big enough for both Hogwash and me to ride him. He helped us advise you during the battle with the Desrai by flying us high into the sky, so we could see where their main forces were.'

'Why is he this small now, then?'

'He shrinks when he doesn't need to use his wings much. It's a way of conserving his energy. If you look closely, you'll see that his wings have grown since this morning,' she said, gently lifting one of them up so that Michael could see.

She was right. They were a few inches larger than they'd been that morning.

'So, if he keeps practising, he'll get bigger again?' he asked.

'Yes, but his full size is still quite small for a dragon. Humans are too big to ride him,' she said.

'Oh,' Michael commented, failing to hide his disappointment. Soaring through the sky on the back of a dragon was something he'd often daydreamed about and now, even though he was in a world where flying, fire-breathing dragons existed, he still wasn't able to do it.

The carriage rolled on smoothly under Hogwash's steady guidance, with the rhythmic clop, clop of the unicorns' hooves making them all sleepy.

They reached the crest of the hill they had been travelling and caught sight of an encampment at the bottom, with tents set up on either side of the road so that travellers could still pass. As Michael looked closer, however, he noticed that the single road now branched into three, one path to the left, one to the right and one straight ahead. A crossroads.

Michael studied the map, and then returned his attention to the crossroads. According to the map's details, there was no hint of a crossroads. In fact, there was no indication that there were any other roads through Treeshallow at all, only footpaths and bridleways, like the one they had to take to reach the mountains. All these paths were dangerous for normal carriages, but Hogwash had told him that theirs had been enforced with magic, protecting its wheels from strain, so an unmade path shouldn't be a problem.

At Michael's word, Hogwash pulled gently on the unicorns' reins and they slowed to a stop, the carriage along with them. 'Did you know this would be here?' Michael asked, jumping out to get a better look. Now that he was closer, he could see that there were people lingering around the tents. 'I can't find anything about it on the map.'

'No,' Hogwash said, frowning. 'It's been a while since we've travelled this road, but the other paths weren't here then. Perhaps the Kingsmen were ordered to expand the road to prevent people travelling across the fields and trampling them.'

'Maybe,' he said uneasily, feeling a gnawing sensation grow in his stomach. Something wasn't right here; the people looked to be too large a party for the number of tents, and they were all wearing strange grey clothing. He picked Small up out of the carriage and put him on his shoulder. Though he was tiny, he was still a dragon, and having him there was reassuring.

As Michael walked nearer, the dragon hissed loudly, and he saw that the grey clothing the people were wearing was not clothing at all; it was skin.

The creatures turned to him and revealed large, round heads and flat ears that hung down by their faces almost like a dog's. Their eyes were small and yellow, and their fingers ended in sharp, hooked nails. Within moments, Michael found that they were charging at him.

'Goblins!' Hogwash shouted, pulling Michael by the robes back up the hill towards the carriage. 'Small, do something!'

The little dragon took flight and circled the goblins. He roared and, taking a deep breath, spat out a wall of flame in front of them. Unfortunately, the flames only reached up to the goblins' legs and they jumped over them with ease. Small tried again, but it was no good. His fire just wasn't powerful enough yet. He looked at Michael despairingly and roared again, diving low over the goblins' heads to try and slow them down at least.

'Get to the side,' Hogwash said, as Hokum jumped out of the

carriage, ready to act before her brother even called her. They ran over to the unicorns and frantically started untying their harnesses. 'We're going to release Lightfoot and Swiftwind. They'll scatter the goblins so that you can trap them with your magic.'

'But I can't use my magic yet!' Michael yelled. The goblins were almost on top of them, and though he had pulled out the stick from inside his robes, it refused to transform into his staff.

'We'll help you,' Hokum said, as she and Hogwash released the last strap holding the unicorns. 'You have to trust us!'

Lightfoot and Swiftwind reared up on their back legs, the blue glow of their horns shining in the goblins' eyes and making them falter. Then they galloped forwards, quicker than any horse Michael had ever seen. Their horns glowed brighter still and encompassed them in blue light, and as they smashed through the crowd of goblins, they sent them flying off in all directions.

'Now, Master!' Hokum said. 'Hold out your staff and say the word "Bind".'

With no time to argue, Michael held out the small stick, almost dropping it as it grew into a tall, twisted staff etched with shimmering runes. 'Bind!' he yelled. A strange sensation pulsed through him and into his staff.

Immediately, the goblins, who had been scattered apart, were now forced together in a large, tight ball, as though they'd been magnetised. None of them could move.

Michael looked on in amazement, and then back at Hogwash and Hokum, who were panting heavily, resting their hands on their knees. The unicorns galloped over to them and touched their heads lightly with their horns. The blue light radiated onto them, and then the two Earth Elves stood up, breathing normally again.

'What happened to you? Were you hurt?' Michael asked them as Small flew down and landed at his feet.

Hogwash shook his head. 'We tired ourselves by using our magic to help you, that's all. Lightfoot and Swiftwind have already replenished our energy; we're fine now.'

'Your magic? Was it you two who made my staff transform?' Michael asked, wishing that he could do it himself. He looked at it, watching it shrink back down to a small stick.

'Yes, it was. That staff is made from a very stubborn wood, and will only transform when you force it to. You're not ready for that yet, so we did it for you,' Hogwash said simply.

'Thank you,' Michael said to them both. Then he regarded Small, Lightfoot and Swiftwind, who were all nudging him affectionately. 'I don't know what I would have done without you three, either,' he added, grinning. He glanced at the ball of goblins. They were shouting at each other and pulling faces. Bound together like that, they looked quite ridiculous, but the terror of their charge had left him feeling uneasy.

'What are they doing here? I thought the goblins lived underground,' he said. Then it occurred to him that no one had told him that, and it wasn't marked on any of the maps he'd looked at. It must have come from Ramble's memory!

'They do, usually,' Hokum said. She went up to the ball of goblins and spoke to them in a language consisting of hisses and popping sounds. Michael listened with interest. He had no idea what they were saying, but it sounded heated.

Eventually, she turned back to them, shaking her head. 'They say that they were chased out of their homes underground by demons. Not the ones we're after, though,' she said quickly as Michael opened his mouth. 'They had too few weapons and weren't aggressive enough. But they were still quite fierce, so the goblins came to the surface instead of trying to fight them. That was two days ago, and they found the Kingsmen building this crossroads by accident. They were hungry, so they tied them up and ate all their food.'

'Then the Kingsmen are still here somewhere?' Michael asked, his eyes scanning the tents.

'Yes, they're all in that big black tent at the end,' Hokum said, pointing to it.

Michael acted before she had even finished speaking. He went up to the ball of goblins and stole a knife he had seen poking out of one's pocket and then sprinted over to the black tent. He cut open the front flaps, which had been laced tightly together, and went in.

Huddled together, filling the tent completely, were men of all ages, wearing crimson and bronze uniforms emblazoned with a gold crown. They were tied up with thick rope, and their mouths had been gagged.

Without hesitating, he took the knife and began cutting their bonds as quickly as he could.

10

THE UNDERONS

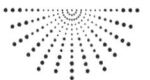

'Thank you, thank you,' an elderly man said, shaking Michael's hand vigorously as the other Kingsmen stood up and stretched.

'No, it was nothing really...' he replied, as the others came up to thank him too, grasping his hands and capturing him in fierce bear hugs.

'I thought we would starve before anyone came to help us,' the old man continued, as Michael clutched at his ribs after a man the size of a gorilla had finally released him from his grip. 'If there's anything we can do to repay you, anything at all, you must ask us. We'll do anything you want.' He turned his fellows and called loudly, 'Right men?' There was a loud shout of agreement as they clapped and cheered, stumbling around as a result of the numbness and pins and needles in their limbs from being tied up so long.

'Who is it we're thanking, Moro? We must ask his name at least, so we can tell the king who saved us,' another man in his late twenties asked.

Before Michael could reply, Hogwash came into the tent and stood by his side. 'You're speaking to our master, the great Wizard

Ramble,' he said proudly, folding his arms and grinning up at Michael. Michael thought he caught an amused tinge to the Earth Elf's voice, but it was so slight he couldn't be sure.

The Kingsmen gasped.

'*The* Wizard Ramble?' the old man, Moro, said. 'The one who vanquished the Desrai eleven years ago?'

'The very same,' Hokum said, edging her way into the tent to stand on Michael's other side.

'Mighty Treeshallow! We must inform the king! He feared that you would never return, sir, and even now is anxious that the demons may come back,' Moro said, clapping his hands together. 'We shall prepare an escort for you at once.'

'Wait,' Michael said, holding up one hand. 'Please, we really don't have time for that. I'm sorry, but we've got to leave soon.'

'Nonsense, Your Wizardship, you shall come with us to see the king!' Moro said, as though Michael had simply been refusing tea.

The Kingsmen hurried outside to make preparations to depart, searching all the other tents for any food that the goblins had spared. They packed it in several wagons that were behind the black tent, chatting merrily to each other despite the short supplies. Some of the younger ones, who had regained their strength after a cup of strong tea and slightly stale cream buns, had managed to dig a large pit to the left of the crossroads. When they were finished, they rolled the ball of goblins into it so that even when Michael's binding spell wore off in a few days, it would still take the creatures hours to make a rope from their clothes to climb out.

'They'll be alright,' Hogwash said, as Hokum watched the goblins glaring back at them from inside the pit. 'You know that they can go without food for two weeks if they have to.'

'I know,' she said, turning away. 'And I suppose they did deserve it, but it wasn't really their fault for being chased out of their homes by the Underons.'

'The Underons?' Michael asked her, as he observed the goblins arguing with each other in their ball. She had told him that most goblins were peaceful creatures who took no notice of humans, content living and working in their own communities underground, but because they had been so afraid, it had made them aggressive. They weren't really bad, they were just frightened. After hearing that, he was glad that he hadn't actually hurt them.

'The Underons are the demons who chased the goblins from their homes. It took me a while to remember their name because they keep a very low profile, but given what the goblins told me, it must have been them. They were once part of the main demon tribe who make up the Desrai. Supposedly, they broke away because they didn't want to continually be at war with humans, wishing to live peacefully instead. But the leader of the demons was so disgusted that he banished them. That's why everyone refers to them as the Underons; it comes from the term "under demons", because they too are enemies of the Desrai,' she replied.

'But if they wanted to stop fighting, then why did they chase the goblins out?' Michael asked her. 'That doesn't make sense.'

'It does if the Desrai were behind it. The Underons won't stay anywhere near them, so if the Desrai are staying where the Underons used to live, then that's why they moved into the goblin caves. They're scared, too,' she said.

'Then what do we do about it? Where did the Underons live?' he said.

'I don't know. They hid themselves away for years, not even coming out to celebrate the defeat of the Desrai.'

'So we still have no idea where they might be?' he said, sighing. One of the Kingsmen was calling him, trying to tell him that they were nearly ready to leave. Small, who had been sniffing around the food, bit the Kingsman on the leg, making the man yelp.

Michael told Small off and turned back to Hogwash and Hokum, ignoring the dragon as he hung his head and rolled upside down on the floor.

'How can we get away from the Kingsmen?' he whispered. 'It takes days to get to the Royal City; we can't waste that much time.'

'Actually, it might be useful to tell the king that the Desrai have appeared again. It won't be much out of our way; the path we need to take to get to the mountains is only a mile or so away from the city,' Hogwash said, watching the Kingsmen mount their wagons.

'But what would I say to him? I've never met a king before,' Michael said, suddenly nervous.

Hogwash smirked. 'By the time we get there, you won't be saying that,' he said, and strode off to get Lightfoot and Swiftwind, who were enjoying being spoilt by the Kingsmen (who'd never seen unicorns before and were giving them more scraps of food than they had room for).

With two wagons in front of them, and three behind, Hogwash drove the carriage on towards the Royal City.

Michael was still dubious about going there instead of straight on to the mountains, but, as Hogwash had pointed out, they weren't even sure if the demons were really up there. Until Small got bigger, he wouldn't be able to fly up to check, and even though he was practising every hour, his wings had only grown a few inches more.

'You're thinking about things too much,' Hokum said beside him.

Michael jumped. He had been so lost in thought that he had forgotten she was there.

'It's only because I want to save Mr Rogers and go back home,' he said.

'Then you're not going to stay here after you save him?' she asked sadly. The question made him uncomfortable.

'Well, I might come back again after I've been home to see my parents,' he said. 'But I can't stay here all the time. I've got to go to school and take my end of year tests.'

'You don't need to go to school now that you're Wizard Ramble. Even when you go back to The Outside, all the knowledge that is beginning to awaken in you will stay there.'

'So I'll be some kind of boy genius?' he asked, grinning at the idea.

'Maybe not a *genius,* but you will find all of your lessons too easy. If you really want to learn, you should go to the Treeshallow library. There are books there about every event that's happened both here and on The Outside. Even the story of the Separation is recorded there,' she said.

'The Separation?' he asked, the name surprisingly familiar.

'The Separation is how Treeshallow and The Outside split apart from each other. It happened so long ago that only someone who has access to the Treeshallow library knows how it occurred. Only those who have been given the key to its doors by the king can enter, and you were given that years ago, even before you defeated the Desrai.'

'Didn't you ask me to go there before to research something?' he said, a vague image entering his head.

'See, your memory *is* coming back,' Hokum said, smiling. 'I wanted you to research the reason why my people became so small. We used to be the same size as humans, but over the years we started shrinking.'

'I'm sorry. I was so busy with everything else that I forgot.'

'I know. It was just before the king asked you for help, so it wasn't your fault.'

Michael looked at her for a moment, and realised that there was something else he remembered. 'Hokum, before I left for The Outside...I gave you something to look after, didn't I?'

'I wondered when you would ask about that. Don't worry, Hogwash and I brought it with us when we moved from the winter house to the summer one. I activated it the minute we knew you were back.'

He relaxed his shoulders, feeling a great relief wash over him.

'You never did tell us what it was for, though,' she said, hoping he'd get her hint.

He didn't, but the answer still decided to pour from his lips before he even realised he knew it. 'Apparently, I'd already planned to transfer my magic. And I also knew that I might have to come back one day. The orb that you activated was an ancient spell that I researched without you and Hogwash knowing.'

'You mean, you did go to the library, then?' she asked.

He scratched his head guiltily. 'Yes, but it was only a few days before I left. You see, the spell that I was researching was one that stopped time.'

'You mean that it's actually *possible?*' she said. 'I had no idea. Even the Fairy Queen who saved Princess Aeros from the Dark Witch's spinning wheel curse had to put everyone to sleep because she didn't think stopping time could be done.'

'It's a very complicated spell, and though I suspected that it was possible, I thought the knowledge behind it must have been lost. I was so surprised when I actually found it that it was all I could do not to run around telling everyone.'

'But what did you use it for? The orb you gave me hasn't stopped time here...' she began, but then the truth came to her. 'It stopped time on The Outside, didn't it?'

Michael smiled. 'The second you activated it, time on The Outside completely froze. My parents probably thought that I'd hung around after class in the school library. I bet they weren't even starting to worry when the spell was activated.'

11
THE ROYAL CITY

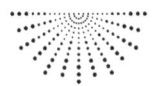

By the dawn of the fourth day journeying to the Royal City, Michael was thoroughly sick of how the Kingsmen were treating him.

He knew they were grateful for being rescued, but there was no need for them to always stop every two hours to make sure he had enough rest, or to give him a larger serving than the others at mealtimes. There were even a few times, when they were nearing a lake or river, that they offered to boil water and fill a tin bath so that he could bathe in comfort instead of swimming in the cold water. Even though he refused each time, they practically undressed him and forced him into it, turning deaf ears to his gasps of pain as the water scorched his skin.

'But, Miss Earth Elf, His Wizardship needs to bathe in warm water to prevent him catching cold,' a slender, dark haired man called Fero said to Hokum after they'd made Michael bathe yet again. She had caught them trying to tip in water that was far too hot and sent them away to cool it first.

'I'm fine washing in the river like everyone else,' Michael said, annoyed at having the same conversation that they'd had the previous day. 'And I don't need extra food, either,' he added, snatching his bowl from the man serving up stew before he could add another ladle full.

'Now, don't be modest, Your Wizardship,' Fero said. 'You require nourishment. There's no need to worry about supplies, either, for there are many farms along the way that I'm sure would be happy to lend us some food.'

From the look on Fero's face, Michael had the distinct impression that he was the one who really wanted to eat good food. But Michael could hardly blame him. After all, Fero and the other Kingsmen had been tied up for two days without any food or water. He could only imagine what that must have been like.

'Alright, but *please* tell me we're nearly there?' he said, sliding his unfinished stew behind him so that Small could eat it. He felt the little dragon lap it up hungrily, almost knocking the bowl over.

'Yes, Your Wizardship. We should get there after noon tomorrow,' Fero replied, bowing low and smiling.

'If we don't keep stopping,' Hogwash muttered as he came to sit by the fire. Fero looked offended and moved away, leaving him and Michael to talk.

'Are you still sure this was a good idea? Surely we could have made it to the mountains by now?' Michael said.

The Earth Elf sniffed suspiciously at his own bowl of stew, wrinkling his nose. 'It's true we could have been well on our way, but do you really think that the king won't seek you out for an audience the moment he hears you've returned?' he said, giving up and passing his bowl to Small, too. 'Besides, it gives Small chance to grow to his full size, not to mention more time for you to practise your magic.'

Michael sighed. 'I suppose you're right. I just can't stand not being able to do anything when Mr Rogers and everyone else here could be in danger.'

'Just try and focus on getting your memories back. Once you fully realise who you are and what you're capable of, I'm sure you'll be able to figure something out. Now, if you'll excuse me, I've got to go and find something to get the taste of that awful stew out of my mouth.'

The next morning dawned with a strong breeze and, feeling the air currents crash against him, Small leapt out of the carriage window and stretched out his wings, riding the wind high up into the sky. Michael grinned as he watched, noticing that the dragon's wings were now double the size they had been when they'd started out, and his body had lengthened too.

'Are you going to send him up to the mountains when he's ready?' Hokum asked, following his gaze.

'I don't know,' Michael replied. 'It depends on what the king says. He might know of the problem by now; Wilhelmina said there was a rumour going around the towns, so perhaps it's spread to the city. If it has, then he may already be preparing his defences.'

She looked at him. As the days had passed, she had seen how he was changing, becoming surer of himself and more alert. When he had first returned to Treeshallow, she had found it easy to believe that he was only a ten-year-old boy on The Outside, but now he was almost the man that Ramble had been before he'd left. 'Do you remember the king now, then?'

Michael grimaced. 'Only too clearly. He's a rash man with a quick temper, who panics at even the smallest thing.'

'Is that really such an unreasonable way to act, given how things were when you last saw him?' she asked.

'I suppose not, but it does make him hard to deal with. It was his fault that the battle with the Desrai went so badly – he wanted to charge in headfirst without a plan. He lost over half his men by doing that, when he could easily have kept casualties to a minimum,' he replied. 'After that, he ran away and hid in his castle, leaving me to deal with it all.'

He could hear the resentment in his voice, but it was too late to hide it. The battle had been meaningless and largely preventable, but the king had taken action too late. No – *Ramble* had taken action too late, for the wizard had known that the demons were stirring up trouble, yet it took the king's plea for help to spur him into doing something about it. So many lives had been snuffed out needlessly; Michael couldn't let that happen again.

Despite Fero's confidence, they didn't reach the thick, golden gates of the Royal City until late evening, after one of the carriages had broken a wheel. It had taken hours to repair it, and then, to Michael's fury, another to prepare food.

By this time, it was all he could do not to throw rocks at them all. He had initially thought about using his magic, as he'd been practising throughout the journey with Hogwash and Hokum's help, but his staff only responded half the time, and even then it was only three quarters of its normal size. However, Hokum had told him, rather firmly, to keep a lid on his temper until after they had seen the king.

Regardless of his sulking, when the gates opened, Michael couldn't help but gape at the lavish streets beyond. They were very similar to cobblestone streets, but the stones laid into them were not plain. They glittered and sparkled like sapphires in firelight.

'I don't remember it being like this,' he said, searching his memories. He knew that some of them were still missing, but even so, he didn't think he could forget something that spectacular.

'It wasn't,' Fero said as he walked level with the carriage window. 'The king had all the streets paved like this as a sign of victory. I heard that he wanted you to be the guest of honour at the ball after their completion, but you had already vanished.'

'I had lots of things to attend to,' Michael said, not completely lying.

Ramble – or himself, he supposed, now that he had most of the wizard's memories – had wanted to leave the Royal City immediately after the battle so that no one would realise how ill it had made him. He'd known that if the king found out, he would have only used it as a reason to keep Ramble in the city, pretending to use his Royal Healers to help him.

'I understand,' Fero said, giving him a mysterious look.

As they entered the city, a great crowd formed on either side of the carriage, still with the wagons in front and behind it. The Kingsmen waved to the people as though they were knights returning from a difficult quest. Michael was puzzled by this, considering that they had only been building the crossroads, but then he recalled Fero telling him that the crossroads were terribly important for traders coming across country. Apparently, there were many dangerous creatures living in the fields and forests between one part of Treeshallow and the next, and the new roads, joining the main one at the crossroads, would mean that they could travel without fear of attack.

He frowned, studying the lavish streets, and then thought back to the simple roads leading off from the crossroads. If the king had so much money to spend on the streets of the Royal City, then why hadn't he had the crossroads built years ago?

Obviously, it wouldn't have been possible before the battle, as the demons would have attacked any Kingsmen they'd seen, but in the years that followed it should have been easy.

'If you grit your teeth any harder, you'll make them crack,' Hokum chided.

'You sound an awful lot like my mother,' Michael said, noticing that he was indeed gritting his teeth, and relaxed his jaws with great difficulty.

'Then I would say that your mother is an exceptionally bright woman,' she replied, grinning at him.

He couldn't help but laugh at her. 'I suppose she is,' he said. 'Though I never really thought about it when I was on The Outside. It's strange, being grown up. Things seem so different, but at the same time, I feel like I've been this age forever.'

'Well, technically, you have. Your magic and memories never age, even when they're passed on to a different body. You'll always be the same age, Wizard Ramble,' she said.

'You say that as though I've been passed into a different body before.'

'That's because you have. It's difficult for me to explain, or even imagine it, but your...essence, shall we say...has been passed to many different people, each with their own personality and traits, yet still unmistakably Wizard Ramble. At one time, I believe that you even trained up apprentices so that they could become the next Ramble,' she told him.

He put a hand to his chin, trying to imagine his mind being passed from body to body, but it was impossible. He hadn't even known about it when Mr Rogers had given him his powers as a baby.

'So, transferring this...essence that makes up Ramble...doesn't that mean that he's immortal?' he asked her.

'Almost. If you had chosen not to change bodies when you were ill, though, you could have died. For some reason or another, no one who has been Wizard Ramble before has ever wanted to die with his powers. They've always chosen to transfer them.'

He gave a small smile. 'It's such a strange idea, jumping from one body to the next...but I think that as long as I don't think about it too much, I suppose it doesn't bother me,' he said, though in truth his mind was reeling.

12

THE KING OF TREESHALLOW

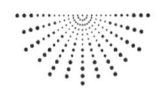

The guards escorted Michael, Hogwash and Hokum into the throne room, an area richly decorated with carvings and sculptures, none showing even the slightest speck of dust. At the back, pronounced against a curtain of deep red, was the throne; a high-backed chair cast completely from iron, decorated with leaves and vines. However, King Albrand was not sitting in it; he was pacing back and forth along the length of the room. His round face was pale and clammy, and small beads of sweat dripped down his pointed nose.

He glanced up as the guards closed the double doors behind them, and let out a noise somewhere between a sigh and a gasp. 'So it's true,' he said, in a breathy voice. 'You've returned to Treeshallow, Wizard Ramble.'

Michael bowed low to the king, hiding the discomfort on his face. The king was exactly how he remembered him; a short, stout man, with an oddly small head compared to the rest of his body. His eyes were dark brown, and they fixed on Michael with an anxious stare.

'Indeed, I have returned, Your Majesty,' Michael replied, straightening himself. 'You're looking well,' he lied.

'Now there's no need for flattery, Ramble. You're already in my good books. I haven't forgotten how you helped me triumph over the demons all those years ago. I'm sure with my aptitude for battle tactics, I would have beaten them back eventually, but there's no denying that you sped up the process,' the king gushed. 'My men also tell me that you saved them from a band of goblins recently.'

'Yes, Your Majesty,' Michael said, clamping his anger down tightly. Never mind that the battle would have been lost if he hadn't stepped in, or that the king had abandoned him and fled to the safety of the castle. It was in the past now; there was nothing he could do about it. 'We happened to be travelling on the road and the goblins attacked us. After I dealt with them, they told us that they had tied up your men in one of the tents,' he continued.

'You can speak goblin?' the king asked, surprised.

'No, but Hokum can,' he said, indicating for her to step forwards so that the king could see her.

'Oh, yes, I'd forgotten you keep a pair of Earth Elves,' the king replied, glancing at her briefly. 'I've always felt that non-humans have no business in human affairs, but I suppose they have their uses. Take my nephew, for example; he's part faun, but he makes a wonderful Bubock root pie. I have always had a soft spot for him though; having a goat woman for a mother can't have been easy. A blessing for him and my idiot brother when she passed, I'm sure.'

Michael sensed Hogwash and Hokum tense up, knowing how furious they were. He bore the same fury at the king's words, but he knew it was useless to confront him, for His Majesty's robes were rippling with ghost spheres, covering them completely. It was the first time he'd seen them attached to anyone in Treeshallow since he'd returned, and he was certain it wasn't a coincidence that the very person he needed to be calm was riddled with them.

'Still, what in Treeshallow were goblins doing above ground?' the king continued, oblivious to the offence he had just caused.

'They were chased out of their homes by the Underons,' Michael said, watching the king keenly for his reaction. He wasn't disappointed, for at the mere mention of the word 'Underons', the king recoiled visibly, the ghost spheres swarming at him as though they meant to choke him.

'The Underons? What do they want?'

'I'm sure you can guess, Your Majesty,' Michael replied, looking the king directly in the eye. 'If I tell you that they, too, were chased away from their home.'

The king swallowed, his bottom lip quivering. 'The Desrai...' he mouthed, unable to speak. The ghost spheres were now covering his face. If Michael didn't do something, then they would start to drive him insane.

He nodded calmly, not wanting to let on to the guards that something was wrong. As long as he didn't give anything away, not even Hogwash and Hokum would suspect anything. 'It appears that they've been quietly building up their ranks, and they've even kidnapped someone from The Outside,' he explained. As he spoke, he discretely reached inside his robes and pulled out the stick, concealing it carefully in his sleeve. He put his hands behind his back and bid it to transform into his staff. He knew it wouldn't do it fully, but he needed whatever power it could give him. 'But there is no need to fear them,' he said, aiming his words not at the king, but at the dense spheres surrounding him. 'I will banish them once again.'

At the word 'banish', he put all his magic into willing the ghost spheres away. There were so many that he wasn't sure he could do it with the little magic he'd been able to practise with, but he felt the spell vibrate through his staff and the spheres all vanished at once. But unlike the reaction that Miss Rowan had had when Mr Rogers banished her ghost spheres, the king remained unchanged.

'Kidnapped someone from The Outside? But why would they do that? This has got nothing to do with The Outside,' he spat, clutching at the hem of his robes as though he would die if he let go.

'The person they took is someone I know,' Michael said, straining his eyes to see if there were any ghost spheres still left. There weren't; he had banished all of them. 'They took him as bait, hoping I would follow them back through the Door Between Worlds into Treeshallow.'

The demons couldn't have known that Michael had no idea who he really was. If Mr Rogers hadn't left the note telling him to go through the Door Between Worlds, then he would probably be at home wondering what on earth had happened in the library. But Mr Rogers had left the note. Maybe he'd done it deliberately to use the Desrai's plans to his advantage, knowing that only Ramble's powers could defeat them. Whatever the reason, what the demons wanted was clear. 'They want to get their revenge on me.'

The king regarded him, his dark eyes narrowed. 'So, this is your fault, is it? Then it is up to you to handle it.' He turned away, muttering under his breath and wringing the hem of his robes fiercely. 'Yes,' Michael heard him say. 'This is the best course of action. Yes, if he fails, then the people will blame him, not me...'

'Your Majesty?' Michael said, as the king's mutterings became incoherent. What was the matter with him? Now that he had rid him of all the ghost spheres, the king should have returned to normal.

'What is it, Wizard? You've had your orders,' the king said, turning to him with wild eyes.

'Forgive me, Your Majesty,' Hogwash said boldly. 'But may I point out that if you had kept up patrols after the battle, then the Desrai wouldn't have had time to build up their ranks again. The way I see it, you're more to blame than our Master. After all, you're the one who requested his help in the battle.'

'Silence!' the king barked at him, so ferociously that the Earth Elf jumped back. The king looked as though he were going to say something else, but Michael stepped forwards, his temper rising again.

'I shall do what I can, Your Majesty,' he said, glaring at the king. 'Though I cannot guarantee that I will succeed,' he added through clenched teeth.

'Is that a threat, Wizard?' the king spat, his eyes going from Michael to Hogwash and Hokum.

'No, Your Majesty. Just a warning,' Michael replied curtly, and then turned his back on the king and strode out the room, shutting the doors behind him with a bang.

As he marched down the corridors of the palace, he was fuming.

'What was that all about?' Hokum asked, trying to keep up with his fast strides. 'What did you need your staff for?'

'So you saw me,' he said, slowing. 'The king was covered in ghost spheres, so I banished them. But it didn't make any difference.'

'What does that mean?' she said, glancing from him to her brother.

Michael shook his head. 'I don't know. There's something wrong with him, but I'm not sure what. And now he's put all the blame for the demons on me. It's suspicious.'

'Then you're not going to fight the Desrai for him?' she asked, catching her breath as he stopped to talk to her.

'Oh, I'll fight them all right, but I *must* find out what's going on here. We're missing something.' He punched the wall with his fist, ignoring the ache in his knuckles. 'If only I had stayed and made sure he sent out regular patrols and dealt with my illness afterwards. Perhaps we wouldn't be in this mess.'

'You would have died if you'd have stayed. You know that,' Hogwash said. 'Besides, what matters now is that you're embracing who you really are.' He grinned. 'You've really grown up these past few days, you know.'

Michael managed a smile. 'I guess you're right. I'm not just a ten-year-old anymore. I'm Ramble of Treeshallow.'

The moment he said it, the stick in his pocket vibrated strongly. He took it out again and watched as it grew in his hand, transforming fully into his staff. It felt different now, no longer temperamental and weak. He could feel the runes etched along it pulsing in his hands, and in that instant, he knew that his full powers had returned along with his memories, and that the staff would obey him properly whenever he needed it.

He looked down at Hogwash and Hokum. They were gazing at him with expressions of deep satisfaction.

'I suppose I just needed to admit it to myself,' he said as his magic pulsed within him. The runes on his staff glowed brighter, and as he stared at it, they began to move about on the wooden surface as if they were alive.

'Would it be inappropriate to say, "We told you so"?' Hogwash said impishly. Hokum hissed at him in disapproval.

Ramble – for now he could no longer call himself Michael – laughed, so loudly that it echoed down the whole corridor. 'I suppose we should enquire about somewhere to stay tonight, shouldn't we? I doubt the king still wants to offer us a room after our little talk.'

They carried on walking and reached the main entrance, finding the Kingsmen all waiting for him.

'So, is the king going to hold a feast in your honour?' Fero asked, standing so close to him that he took several involuntary steps backwards.

'I'm afraid the king has more pressing things to attend to,' Ramble said. 'He also asked me to carry out an important task for him, so I'm afraid that I can't stay here much longer.'

Fero's face fell. 'Well, I'm sure he rewarded you in another way,' he said, trying to be cheerful, but as he looked at Ramble he knew that the king had done no such thing. 'You're welcome to come to dinner at my house. My wife makes a wonderful Bubock root pie...'

'Thank you for the offer, Fero, but I'm afraid I really do need to attend to the king's business first.'

PART II
RAMBLE

13

PRINCESS HURELLA

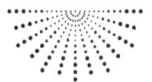

Ramble said goodbye to the Kingsmen and left the palace along with Hogwash and Hokum, hearing the great double doors close behind them with a clang. The guards outside tipped their helmets to him, a questioning look in their eyes, but he ignored them and made his way down the steep staircase to the city streets below. He was walking so quickly that again Hogwash and Hokum had trouble keeping up, but before he could reach the bottom, someone called out.

They turned to see a young woman standing there, dressed in a long silken tunic and flowing trousers. Her hair was silver, almost the colour of Lightfoot and Swiftwind's coats, and was so long it reached down to her ankles.

'I'm sorry my father was so rude to you,' she said. 'It seems he's forgotten how you saved me from the disease that nearly ruined this city. If it wasn't for you, I don't think I would be standing here right now.'

As she spoke, Ramble's eyes widened. A memory was beginning to surface, showing a young girl with hair as silver as hers. 'Princess Hurella?'

'Yes,' she said, the corners of her mouth inching up. 'It's been a long time, hasn't it, Wizard Ramble?'

'It has. You were only a child when I saw you last,' he said warmly. Her eyes were soft and she wore a gentle expression. 'You look like your mother, princess. I'm sure she would be proud if she could see you now.'

To his surprise, she frowned. 'If she could see me now, then she would have kept my father under control all these years,' she said. 'I don't blame you for her death, you know. You tried everything you could. The disease was just more advanced in her than it was with me.'

'Thank you,' he said, remembering the day he'd had to tell the king that his queen had passed away. She had been a caring, sensible woman, who would have been able to prevent the battle between the Desrai and the people of Treeshallow as easily as breaking up a squabble among children.

It was the upset caused by her death that made King Albrand lose all rational thought. He had deliberately provoked the Desrai into war, after hearing a rumour that the disease had been caused by a rogue band of demons. Supposedly, they'd attacked one of the city's royal guards with a cursed blade and the disease spread from there, running riot throughout the city until over half the population had caught it. However, the rumour had never been proven, and the guard in question died before he could confirm anything.

'I heard the conversation that you had with my father. Are the Desrai really back?' she asked, drawing her arms around her in the chill air.

'We believe so; there's no way they would try something as risky as kidnapping someone from The Outside if they didn't have the numbers to back it up. But I haven't managed to locate them yet. I might be able to soon, though, if Small thinks he's ready to fly long distances again.'

'Small?' she asked. 'You mean Small the dragon? Is he here?'

She glanced around eagerly, looking so much like the little girl he remembered that he laughed at her. 'What's so funny?' she said, pouting.

'Nothing,' he lied. 'And Small isn't here, he's back where we left our carriage. Lightfoot and Swiftwind are with him, if you'd care to come and see them?'

'May I?' she asked, her eyes lighting up.

'You're a princess; I don't believe I can refuse you,' he said. 'But perhaps I'd better fetch you a cloak first.'

He tapped his staff on the ground three times and waited. The princess looked confused, but he pointed upwards at the palace and as she followed his gaze, she saw a window open in the top tower. Out of it came a deep red cloak, trimmed with gold thread. It floated down and landed gently in her outstretched hands.

'This is my little red roaming cloak,' she said. 'I haven't worn it for years.'

'I'm afraid it's the only one I recall you wearing, so that's all I could summon,' he said. 'I've made it larger, so it should fit you still.'

She stared at Ramble in amazement, running her fingers over the dense fabric. She tried it on; it fit her perfectly.

'I don't think he was able to do that before,' Hogwash whispered to his sister as they followed behind them along the streets towards the carriage.

'No,' Hokum whispered back. 'He didn't use any words at all.'

Ramble heard her and gave a mysterious smile. 'When I read about other wizards in stories, I always preferred the ones who could use magic without saying anything. That's why I thought I'd try it,' he said, out of the princess's earshot. 'It's fun, but my magic is stronger doing things the usual way.'

Hogwash and Hokum glanced at each other. There was a confidence in Ramble that they'd rarely encountered.

When they reached the carriage, the princess let out a girlish squeal and ran over to Lightfoot and Swiftwind, burying her face in their manes. 'They were only foals when I last saw them,' she said. 'I'm so glad I got to see them again.'

The unicorns nuzzled her back, pawing the ground with their hooves. On top of the carriage, the sleeping figure of Small stirred at the sound of her voice. He stood up and stretched his wings, peering over the side. His purred as he saw her and sprang down, knocking her to the ground.

'Be careful, Small,' Ramble chided, helping the princess up. Small ignored him and licked her face instead.

'I've missed you too, Small,' she said, wiping his saliva off her cheeks. 'But I remember you being bigger than this.'

'You must have seen him during the battle. When he needs to fly for a long time, he grows large enough to carry Hogwash and Hokum on his back. When he doesn't, he returns to being no bigger than my head,' he explained. Even though the two Earth Elves had told him this earlier, he now remembered it. No longer was it strange for him to talk about things he recollected from the previous Ramble; they felt just like the memories he had as Michael, memories that really were his.

'But now we need him to fly again,' he continued, 'so he's been trying to grow back to his full size.'

'So he's naturally small?' she said, rubbing the dragon's scaly head.

'He's still a baby. Dragons don't become adults until they're two hundred years old, when they're able to maintain their full size. Small's only seventy eight, and even when he does become an adult, he won't be much bigger.'

'Why not?' the princess asked curiously. 'I thought dragons grew to the size of mountains.'

'They usually do, but Small is from a dragon clan who only grow to the size of a donkey at their biggest. Their size makes them fast fliers, so hardly anyone ever sees them.'

He looked up at the sky and saw that the moon had risen high. 'I'm afraid that I must take you back now, princess,' he said. 'I have to find somewhere to stay for the night that has a stable large enough for Lightfoot and Swiftwind.'

'I think I might know of a place,' the princess said. 'It's very expensive, but if I go with you, then they might let you stay for free.'

'I can't do that,' he objected. 'It's not fair to the owners.'

'Then I'll pay for you out of father's funds,' she said, and strode off into the night before he could refuse.

Sighing, he took hold of the unicorns' reins and led them after her. Even though it was late, there were still plenty of people about enjoying the city's evening market. All the stalls were lit by candles; some with strong scents and multicoloured flames, while others were carved to look like trees, with flames coming out of each branch.

Everyone watched them as they went past, glancing from Ramble to the unicorns, and then at the princess. Hogwash and Hokum had decided to ride in the carriage with Small, remembering only too well that the sight of two Earth Elves in the Royal City had had tongues wagging for weeks.

The inn that the princess led them to looked like a smaller version of the palace. The only difference was that it lacked the great staircase leading up to the main doors, and there was a sign hanging outside that said, 'The Dancing Donkey'. Ramble frowned at the name; it was another reminder that the stories on The Outside originated in Treeshallow, growing distorted and warped in the dreams of the authors, even those from his father's favourite author.

'What's the matter?' Princess Hurella asked him, seeing his expression.

'It's nothing, I just wasn't expecting anything this grand,' he said. 'Not that there's anything wrong with it,' he added hastily as her face fell.

'As long as you don't mind it, then,' she said, and took him inside so that they could speak to the innkeeper.

They were greeted instantly by a blast of warm air and the scent of chestnuts. The atmosphere was so different from the inn's outside appearance that he thought for a moment they had ended up in a different inn altogether. It was only when he looked up at the ceiling and saw it was decorated with paintings of donkeys that he realised he was wrong.

    Large, squashy armchairs filled one side of the room, with plain wooden serving tables at the other. A black stove stood in the middle tended by a woman in a patchwork dress. She was humming loudly as she checked the contents within it, pausing to watch them come in. Her eyes narrowed.

14
SMALL TAKES FLIGHT!

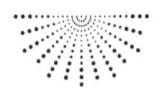

'Are you the innkeeper?' Princess Hurella asked the woman.

'I am,' she replied harshly, taking in the princess's red cloak, hooded over so that it obscured her face. 'But we don't serve Walking Wolves in here. There's a place on the outskirts of the city that caters specifically to your kind. You might try there.'

Princess Hurella laughed and pulled back her hood. The woman's face paled. 'Your Highness, you must forgive me,' she stammered, curtseying awkwardly. 'I saw the red of your cloak and...well, you know that the Walking Wolves always wear red hoods...'

'It's quite alright, I understand,' the princess said. 'But if a Walking Wolf were to come in here, you needn't be so curt with them. The legend about them devouring old ladies and gentlemen was proven to be complete hearsay fifteen years ago.'

'Ah, yes, I remember now, Your Highness,' the innkeeper said, curtseying again as though she wasn't sure what else to do. 'It's just that I've always had a fear of wolves.' She faltered, seeing the princess waiting patiently to do business.

The princess smiled and indicated for Ramble to step forwards.

'This is my dear friend Ramble,' she said. 'For reasons that I cannot say, he is unable to stay at the palace. I had hoped that there would be room for him here.'

'Oh, yes, Your Highness. We have plenty of rooms available. Some of them even have their own private bathroom,' the innkeeper replied. 'Would he be staying here...free of charge?'

'Not at all,' the princess said. 'The Crown will cover all expenses. I believe he requires the use of your stables too, if possible.'

'You have horses, sir?' the innkeeper asked, turning to him.

'Actually, they're unicorns. And I have a carriage as well, if you have space for it. I've got a dragon with me too, but he's small enough to stay in the room if you'll permit him to. My friends here will also be sharing the room,' Ramble said, stepping aside so that she could see Hogwash and Hokum, who had climbed up onto a stool to look around the inn properly.

The woman swallowed several times. 'Of course, elves of all races are welcome. But did I hear you correctly when you said that you had unicorns and a dragon?' she asked, her voice weak.

'Yes. There's not a problem, is there?' he said.

'Oh, no sir,' she replied quickly. 'I'm surprised, is all. I don't usually get many people travelling with unicorns or dragons, or even Earth Elves, come to that. I've had Wind Elves and Fire Elves, and even a few Water Elves, but never any Earth Elves. I thought they always preferred to keep to themselves?'

'Hogwash and Hokum have special circumstances,' he said, grinning back at them. 'They're my permanent companions.'

'I see,' the innkeeper said. 'If you give me a few minutes, I will see to your accommodation, then.' With that, she bustled off into a side room.

'Why do I have the feeling that by tomorrow morning, everyone in Treeshallow will know where I'm staying?' he said to the princess, sighing deeply.

'And why should you mind about that?' she asked.

'You *are* a famous wizard,' Hokum pointed out, agreeing with her.

'No one has seen you for ten years. Now that you're back, the people are bound to be interested. Besides, no other wizards have unicorns, dragons and elves at their side. In some ways, you represent all the different races in Treeshallow.'

'It's true,' Hogwash said with a nod. 'No other wizards have ever understood the other races like you do.'

'I suppose so,' Ramble began, 'but how am I supposed to deal with the Desrai and rescue Mr Rogers without causing a panic if everyone is interested in what I'm up to?'

'Let me deal with that,' the princess said, tapping the side of her nose.

The innkeeper came back and told them that she had a room perfect for their needs, and that there was plenty of space in the stables for Lightfoot and Swiftwind, as well as the carriage. 'Will you be having dinner, sir?' she asked. 'There's not much left at this time of night, but I'm sure I can find you something.'

'Yes, thank you,' he replied. 'Are you eating here too, princess?'

'I've already eaten,' she said. 'Besides, Father will be wondering where I am by now. Hopefully he hasn't sent out the royal guards yet. It's always embarrassing to have them escort me back.'

After telling the innkeeper that she would get her money the next day if she called at the palace, the princess said goodnight to them all and left them alone. They checked that Lightfoot and Swiftwind had been taken to the stables properly and given their own dinner, then fetched Small inside and sat down to eat the homemade stew that the innkeeper served them.

When they were finished, the innkeeper led them up to the top of a very long, spiral staircase (always keeping one eye on Small as though he would suddenly set everything on fire), and stopped outside the only door. Unlocking it, she directed them through. The room beyond was circular, and furnished with soft blue carpet and heavy curtains, with a tapestry depicting the royal family tree on one of the walls. There was a long double bed inside, as well as two single ones and what appeared to be an extra large dog bed for Small. There was also a trapdoor that led down into a private bathroom, with a large bath, a sink and, to everyone's joy after being on the road for so long, a proper toilet.

They thanked the innkeeper for her time and watched as she left, closing the door softly behind her with a click.

'If you two don't mind,' Ramble said to Hogwash and Hokum, 'I think I'll have a bath.'

'Take your time,' they both replied, not really paying attention. They were staring at the single beds with dismay; noting that there weren't even any house plants for them to climb in to sleep. Ramble put a hand to his chin. That wouldn't do. They hadn't slept in a human bed for so long that even if they tried, they probably wouldn't get any rest at all.

He stepped over to the window and looked outside. Below him was the inn's courtyard, leading to the stables. It was lit by a street lantern, and in its light he could see two small trees in pots at either side of the stables' entrance. They weren't much, but they were better than nothing. Carefully, he opened the window and pointed at them with his staff. 'Transport,' he said, and before he could step back out of the way, the trees came hurtling into the room. Branches scraped against him and one of the heavy pots crashed into his leg, but then the trees floated gently down onto the floor. 'Are these any better?' he asked the two Earth Elves.

'Mighty Treeshallow!' Hogwash cried. 'These are young Goldus trees. They're very rare, and very expensive, but their branches are strong and fragrant. I've only seen one once before; it grew golden apples the size of my head.'

'They're wonderful,' Hokum added, 'but are you sure the innkeeper won't mind you taking them like that?'

'I'm sure we can come to an agreement if I tell her that they're more suitable for you to sleep in than beds. Now, about that bath...' he said, and opened the trapdoor into the bathroom. Small, who had been investigating the dog bed, looked up hopefully.

'Dragons don't need baths, Small,' Hogwash told him firmly. The little dragon hung his head and turned the dog bed upside down so that he could lie under it.

'We'll turn down your bed so it's ready for when you come out. Please take your time,' Hokum called down to Ramble.

He poked his head back up through the hole, his brow creased. 'You don't always have to do everything for me.'

'But we've always done it,' she said, looking at him curiously.

'I know that,' he said, flicking through his memories. 'I just don't think it's right. It makes me feel like you're my servants.'

'We are your servants, though,' Hogwash protested. 'We've been your servants ever since you rescued us. We're happy to be.'

Ramble sighed. 'If that's what you want. But perhaps you should think about us being friends instead,' he said, ducking back through the hole and closing the trapdoor behind him.

'I think that he must have been a very kind boy on The Outside,' Hokum commented quietly to her brother.

'I think you're right,' Hogwash agreed.

In the morning, after the best night's sleep any of them had had since leaving the summer house, Ramble woke to find Small lying above his head, stretched out on his pillows.

The dragon was now as long as the bed was wide, and his wings had grown to match. As soon as he realised Ramble was awake, Small licked the wizard's face happily, unfolding his wings to show off their full width.

'So you've finally reached your full size,' Hokum said, watching them from the branches of her Goldus tree. 'Considering how lazy you've been all these years, you've managed it quickly.'

Small gave a sniff, sending up a small stream of smoke from his nostrils.

'Do you think you can make it to the mountains now?' Ramble asked, stroking the dragon's scaly neck.

Small gave an energetic nod, and leapt off the bed to fly around the room, landing by the window. Ramble grinned at him and got up to open it. The moment he did, the dragon scrambled onto the ledge.

'Just have a good look around,' Ramble told him. 'If you see the demons, don't try to land. Come back straight away; I don't want you getting hurt.'

Small gave another nod and licked him on the face again, before leaping out of the window, extending his wings to catch the wind and gliding off into the distance.

'He'll be alright, won't he?' Ramble said, turning to Hogwash and Hokum.

'He's a dragon, he'll be fine,' Hogwash said, stifling a laugh. 'He might be a baby, but he can still breathe fire. He's much more powerful now than he was when we came across the goblins.'

'I hope you're right,' Ramble replied.

15

GOSSIP AND RUMOURS

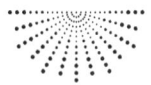

'Well, we can't just sit here and wait,' Ramble said, stretching. He searched through his bags for fresh robes.

'What do you plan to do, then?' Hogwash asked, as he and Hokum automatically began making the bed. Ramble rolled his eyes at them. He was perfectly capable of making it himself.

'Gather information,' he replied, going over to the dressing screen and standing behind it so that he could get changed in private.

'Do you really think any of the city people know what's going on?' Hogwash asked him. 'I didn't see any sign of panic.'

Ramble came out from behind the screen, adjusting his clean robes. 'Just because the king hadn't heard anything, doesn't mean that other people haven't. It looks like there are lots of traders here at the moment; who knows what they've seen or heard?'

After a hot breakfast of Bubock root pie, the three of them emerged into the city streets, eager to gather whatever information they could. Despite Lightfoot and Swiftwind's enthusiasm, Ramble had to leave the unicorns in the stables. He knew they would draw too much attention and prevent any chance he had of eavesdropping.

Listening in to conversations wasn't something he liked doing, but to ask the people directly about the demons would only cause alarm.

If everyone was afraid, then the city and most of Treeshallow would turn to chaos, and if he really did have to fight the Desrai again, then he preferred it to be somewhere where he could think properly and not get distracted.

As they walked down the streets towards the main market, Ramble thought back to the previous battle. It was confusing at first, because the memory of being there and the memory he had of reading about it kept crossing over, but eventually he was able to separate them out.

He remembered the closeness of the king's army surrounding him, facing the demons as they charged in masses towards them. The Desrai had been at least ten thousand strong, while the king's army were a mere two thousand, three hundred and seventy-eight. The king, fitted into his full armour, had ridden proudly onto the battlefield with him, giving his men a pep talk about courage and valour, only to flee upon seeing so many of his soldiers cut down and realising that there was little hope of winning against so many.

That was why the battle had fallen apart. Once the men had seen their king run, they lost the will to fight and fell back, leaving only Ramble to face the horde. He'd had no choice but to use the full force of his magic, casting a wall of solid flame that spat out molten arrows. The demons hadn't been prepared for anything so lethal, and such was the speed at which Ramble had raised it, nearly all of them had been wiped out before they could comprehend what had happened.

It had been that strong surge of magic that had made him ill, disrupting the flow inside him so that it started rejecting his body.

'Ramble, are you listening?'

He blinked and looked down at Hokum as she studied his face with concern. 'Are you alright?' she asked. 'You've gone pale.'

Ramble swallowed, feeling that his throat had gone dry. 'I'm fine,' he said. 'I was thinking about...last time.'

She put her hand on his thigh consolingly, unable to reach any higher. 'It won't be like that this time. As soon as we find out where they are, we can head off any sign of war before it even gets started.'

'You're right,' he said, giving himself a good shake.

They turned a corner and found themselves in a street full of stalls of every kind and colour, stretching as far as they could see. There was a black stall with yellow stripes to their right, selling honey and beeswax candles, and to their left was one which was deep purple, selling various creams and powders. One of the packets was labelled 'Anti-Wart Powder' and was advertised as being perfect for good witches who wanted to avoid looking like stereotypes of their wicked counterparts.

As Ramble read the other labels, a woman with a greenish tinge to her skin and six extremely large warts on her chin came up to the stall and studied the powders and creams with interest. The vendor, a tall, stout woman, smiled at her.

'Ah, Baltinda! It's good to see you again. How's the anti-envy cream coming along?' she asked.

'Well, as you can see, my skin is gradually fading back to its natural colour now. I can't believe I was involved with that coven for so long that my skin turned green! I only went there for a laugh, I never thought I'd start becoming a wicked witch like the rest of them,' the green-tinged woman replied.

'Ah, you can't help things like that. Wicked witches are very clever at deceiving good witches. I think Wilhelmina is the only good witch I've ever known not to be lured by their charms.'

'Oh, don't talk to me about Wilhelmina. She's so full of good spirits that it makes me sick,' the woman spat in disgust. Ramble noticed that her green skin darkened slightly as she spoke.

'Now there's no need to upset yourself, Baltinda. Here, have some more anti-envy cream,' the vendor said, handing her a large jar of it.

'Thank you,' the witch said, taking it quickly and spreading some on her cheeks. The green diluted within seconds. 'I know I shouldn't carry on, but have you heard that she's made friends with Ramble now that he's come back?'

'No, I haven't. What's she up to then, I wonder? I knew that she'd met him a few times before, but they were never very—'

The vendor stopped as she caught sight of Ramble looking over the witch's shoulder. Seeing her stare, the witch turned around. She let out a small cry and stepped back, knocking several packets off the stall. Ramble bent down and picked them up, handing her one of them.

'Here,' he said. 'I believe you need this one.'

The witch looked down at the packet he'd given her. It was the anti-wart powder. 'I—' she began, but before she could say anymore, he gave a curt wave and turned away to merge with the crowd.

'I thought you didn't want to attract attention?' Hogwash said to him after they had gone quite a distance.

'I don't,' Ramble replied. 'But I can't stand idle gossip, especially when it's about someone I know.'

'But we're here for gossip,' Hokum pointed out as they made their way over to a stall that sold various types of weapons.

'That's different,' Ramble said stubbornly.

Hokum looked as though she were about to say something else, but then he saw her ears twitch and she put a finger to her lips. She signalled for him to look at the vendor at the weapon stall, who was deep in conversation with a tall man in armour.

'I heard they're hiding in the swamps, biding their time,' the man in armour was saying, but the vendor shook his head.

'If there were any demons in the swamps, then the Bog dragons would have told us, or chased them out themselves. The Bog dragons hate the demons as much as we do,' he said.

'The Bog dragons are big and slow, and their eyesight isn't very good. If the demons found a place to hide well enough, then the Bog dragons wouldn't even know they were there,' the man in armour protested.

'Well, I just can't see them being there, especially if they really have kidnapped someone from The Outside like I've heard,' the vendor replied.

'They kidnapped someone from The Outside? Does the king know?' the man in armour gasped.

'I don't know, but now that Ramble's back, I think the king'll dump the whole situation on him,' the vendor said, rubbing his chin.

'You know that's bordering on treason, disrespecting the king like that?' the armoured man said.

The vendor laughed. 'What do you care? You moan about the king every day,' he said. 'Anyway, I'd say the demons are hiding near the Door Between Worlds. I know it's near a town, but there are lots of places for them to hide out there.'

'Like what? I heard it's just plain fields over that way,' the armoured man said.

'Ah, but that's where they buried all those wardrobes, isn't it? If they managed to dig up one of those, then they could be hiding in it. The space within them is rumoured to be so big that the entire palace could fit inside. That's why the king's grandfather banned them in the first place. He didn't want his enemies getting their hands on them and hiding inside, ready to spring an attack at any moment.'

'I highly doubt that those wardrobes still work after all these years, even if the demons did manage to find one. If the stories are true, then the space inside them was very temperamental. One of them kept leading people out into a snow covered forest miles away from anywhere.'

Ramble narrowed his eyes. He had heard about those wardrobes before, but he hadn't known they were buried near the Door Between Worlds. If it was true, and they did still work, then that could change everything. There was only one person he knew who might be able to confirm it: Wilhelmina.

16

CONTACT LOCATE

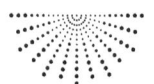

Moving into a side alley out of sight from the market goers, Ramble took the wooden stick out of his robes and transformed it into his staff, resting it gently on his brow. 'Contact Locate,' he whispered, imagining Wilhelmina's face. His staff wasn't strictly necessary, but with the hubbub from the market, he wanted as clear a connection as he could manage.

Immediately, her voice rang in his ears. 'Hello?'

'Wilhelmina, it's Ramble,' he said, going further back into the alley to make sure he wouldn't be overheard.

'Ramble? So, you're finally calling yourself that again?' It sounded like she was smiling.

'Yes, my memories came back to me. Listen,' he said, dropping his voice even lower. 'I'm in the Royal City, and I've heard some rumours about the Desrai.'

'You're in the Royal City?' she repeated. 'I thought you were going to investigate the mountains.'

'We were invited here by some Kingsmen we rescued on the road. They'd been attacked by goblins. Please,' he said, getting to the point.

'Have you ever heard about the magic wardrobes that lead into rooms so large it's possible to hide an army inside?'

'As a matter of fact, I have heard of them. My great grandmother used to have one, until they were banned. They were made of wood from the Forest of Ainran, I believe. Her one always malfunctioned though, and one of the cauldrons she put in there ended up by the Everlasting Lantern Inn, on the edge of the forest. She suspected that it was something to do with the wood wanting to return to Ainran, but she could never prove it,' she replied. 'You know, my grandmother had quite the cauldron shop. She even sold one to the three prophet sisters, around the time of—'

'Wilhelmina,' he cut in, trying to hold back his irritation. 'Do you know if the wardrobes were buried near the Door Between Worlds?'

'Oh...Now that you mention it, I do believe they are. Someone told me that they were buried in the field that you must have come out in when you came through the door,' she said. 'Why do you ask?'

He took in a deep breath, casting his eyes around for eavesdroppers. 'One of the vendors I overheard at the market said that he thought the Desrai had dug up one of those wardrobes.'

'Hmm,' Wilhelmina said.

'What is it?' Ramble asked her, noticing a suspicious tone in her voice.

'If they did manage to dig one up, then it's very likely that they'd use it to hide in. But I don't see how they could have done that and gone unnoticed. The field is in full view of the town; if we'd seen demons about, we would have sent our best mages out to ward them off. We haven't seen any activity in that field at all, though.'

Ramble thought, rubbing his head with his staff. 'What if they did it after the battle? Everyone was celebrating for at least two weeks afterwards. Any activity could have easily gone unnoticed.'

'But I thought that the few remaining demons retreated to the mountains at the time?'

'It's possible that a handful might have gone the other way, to the Door Between Worlds,' he said. 'Still, this is all speculation; I can't do anything until Small gets back from the mountains. If the demons aren't there, then I'll need to investigate that field.'

'Well, I'll ask around and see if anyone knows anything over here. If I do hear anything, I'll use "Contact Locate" to let you know,' she said, and then her voice was gone.

He straightened up and took his staff away from his head, shrinking it back to a small stick again before putting it back in his pocket. He gazed out at the busy market and sighed, but then heard a tapping sound by his feet. Glancing down, he saw that both Hogwash and Hokum were tapping their feet impatiently.

'What's the matter?' he asked them.

Hogwash gave him an exasperated look. 'We were wondering if you were going to tell us what she said.'

Ramble rubbed the back of his neck guiltily. 'Sorry, I always forget that you can't hear the full conversation with that spell,' he said. 'Apparently the wardrobes are buried there, but she doesn't think it would have been possible for the demons to dig any up without being spotted by the townspeople.'

'So there's no chance that they've got one, then?' Hogwash said, running his hands through his short hair.

'I'm not sure. If they attempted it not long after the battle when everyone was celebrating, then it's possible that no one saw them. That would have allowed them to build up their ranks in secret. But then the same could be said if they stayed in the mountains; it's well known that humans rarely set foot there.'

'Then let's hope that Small stays safe,' Hokum said, casting her gaze in the direction of the mountains. Their peaks were just visible over the tops of the buildings; the snow on top reflecting the bright sun.

They carried on wandering around the market, eavesdropping on as many conversations as they could, and though they found out nothing new, there were many whispers about the kidnapping of Mr Rogers. Most of the people were surprised that the demons would go that far, and their conversations were becoming progressively more tense.

An elderly woman started whispering that the demons were going to bring more people from The Outside, and that the kidnapping of Mr Rogers had merely been a test to see if it were possible. She said that their goal was to cause a conflict between the people from The Outside and Treeshallow, and that the people from The Outside were too stupid and easy to manipulate to see through it.

Ramble had almost stepped in to state that the people on The Outside weren't much different from people in Treeshallow, but Hogwash stamped on his foot before he could say anything. 'I thought the idea was only to listen,' he hissed, shaking his head at the wizard.

'Sorry,' Ramble said meekly, limping away from the woman. 'I forgot. I'm not sure that letting rumours like that spread around the city is a wise idea, though.'

Hokum laughed softly beside him. 'You don't need to worry so much,' she said. 'The other market goers avoided her completely; I doubt if even one of them took her words seriously.'

'You're right,' a voice said behind them, making them all jump. It was Princess Hurella. She was clad in her red cloak, and her cheeks were pink from the chill morning air. 'Her name is Matil, and everyone around here knows that she tells tall tales all the time.'

'Then there's no danger that the things she's saying will start a panic?' Ramble asked.

'Only if someone like my father hears her, but as you saw, most people ignore her. I doubt you'll have much of a problem,' she replied calmly. 'So, how goes your search for the whereabouts of the Desrai?'

'We sent Small off to the mountains this morning, and we've been listening to the people here to see if there's any news, but there's nothing definite yet.'

'Small's gone already?' she said. 'But he was still so little when I saw him yesterday.'

'He reached his full size overnight,' Ramble said proudly. 'Don't worry, I told him not to land if it was dangerous.' He paused and looked at her curiously. 'Why are you here, by the way?'

The princess lowered her eyes. 'Actually, it's about father,' she said. 'He's locked himself in his chambers, and refuses to let anyone in.'

Ramble frowned. So the madness that held the king was still there. 'Did he say why?' he asked her.

She shook her head. 'No one's been able to get any sense out of him since you left the palace,' she said. 'Do you think someone's put a curse on him?'

'A curse?' he said, narrowing is eyes. If someone had cursed the king, then that would explain why he hadn't returned to normal after the ghost spheres had left. But why would someone want to do that? Not to mention how – there were plenty of spells set up within the palace to prevent that very thing. Some of them he'd even put there himself, before the king's coronation forty-five years ago.

'Do you think you can get me back into the palace?' he asked her.

'I think so. Father hasn't officially ordered anyone to keep you out. No one knows what you spoke about except me, so they don't know why he's upset with you,' she said.

'Good. I want to try and speak to him immediately. If he is cursed, or under any kind of spell, then I need to break it quickly.'

The princess saw the seriousness in his eyes. Not wanting to waste any time, she took them all back to the palace straight away, going through the side entrance to avoid the enormous staircase at the front.

The door they went through came out into the kitchens, which were full of the smells of lunch being prepared. Chefs and their assistants bustled about, shouting to each other about food that wasn't presented properly or needed more cooking time.

None of them took any notice as they passed; most of them were too busy to even look up. 'You must go through here often,' Ramble said, as they took a small door into another kitchen, this one full of dessert chefs.

'This is the route I take when I don't want to be followed. If I go out the front entrance, then I always end up with my maidservants and the royal guards chasing after me. This way is much easier; I simply tell them that I have a headache and go to my room. There's a dumbwaiter in there that leads straight here, and for some reason they never think that I'll use it,' she said, hurrying through yet another door, this time to the serving room.

They saw a dumbwaiter over to one side, with a trolley laid out with mid-morning tea next to it, ready to be sent up.

'Don't worry,' she said, going past it. 'I'm not going to make you go up in it. Besides, if I stepped out of my room with a wizard and two Earth Elves, I'd get a lot of funny looks. The maids already gossip about me enough as it is.'

17

THE KING'S MADNESS

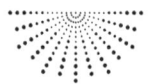

Princess Hurella led them out of the serving room and into the hall, taking them to a spiral staircase leading up to the palace's main floor.

They went past the throne room and into a side corridor where a large, elaborate tapestry made up of rich red and gold thread hung on the wall. The princess stopped in front of it, facing a part depicting a man kneeling by a giant tree, holding up a cushion with a crown nestled in the middle.

She lifted the tapestry and tapped the wall behind it rhythmically. There was a grinding sound and part of the wall opposite them opened inwards, revealing a passageway. They went inside, following it to its end, and found a small door with a rusted padlock.

'Father's room lies beyond this door. We wouldn't have been allowed through the main doors, and this is the only other entrance. He doesn't know about it, so I knew there wouldn't be any guards here. We should be safe; I think it comes out at the back of his closet,' she whispered.

'Why is it locked if he doesn't know about it?' Ramble asked.

'It's always been locked. I think my grandfather might have done it, or even his father. I've never managed to get it open, so...' she said, looking at him hopefully.

'I'm no expert at picking locks, but I'll see what I can do,' he said. He whipped out his staff and placed the tip of it against the lock. 'Break,' he whispered.

The lock rattled for a moment, and then fell to pieces on the floor. 'It must have been old, I hardly used any force at all.' He touched the handle and pulled it hard. The door creaked and showered them with a cloud of dust, disturbing several spiders that quickly scuttled away out of sight. He pulled again, and this time it swung open, revealing a room dedicated entirely to fancy doublets and robes, and a surprisingly large collection of shoes.

'Ha!' the princess said, 'I was right! I always knew that this part of the closet wall looked strange.'

They marched through the king's closet and opened the mirrored door at the end. It swung open easily and they stepped out into the king's bedroom, taken up almost entirely by the enormous bed in the centre. The king was lying in it, huddled up between his pillows, and clutching the covers around him tightly. He was still wearing his crown, but it was now lopsided and hanging over one of his eyes, which bulged incredulously when he saw Ramble enter the room. He lifted a shaking finger, a mix of anger and fear on his face. 'What are you doing here, Wizard? You won't get any help from me. No, sir, you will not!'

The ghost spheres that Ramble had banished had returned, numbering even more that before. But now he saw that it wasn't the king they were attracted to, it was something else.

'Father, stop being so ridiculous,' Princess Hurella said angrily. 'Ramble isn't here to ask for your help. He's here to *give* you help.'

'I don't need any help,' the king snapped.

'I'm afraid I have to disagree, Your Majesty,' Ramble said, stepping closer. 'Locking yourself in your rooms and refusing to open the doors for anyone is absurd behaviour, even for someone as cowardly as you.' The princess shot him a questioning look, but he shook his head. There would be time to question his methods later.

'Cowardly! *Cowardly?* How dare you!' the king hissed at him.

'But you are, Your Majesty,' Ramble said coolly. 'You fled at the battle, causing your men to lose hope and retreat, and yesterday, at the mere mention of the Desrai, you turned to shambles and blamed me for the situation. While I am partly to blame, these circumstances could have easily been avoided if you'd have taken action when it was needed.'

'You're lying! I did not flee at the battle, I stood proud until the very end,' the king objected, sending spittle flying everywhere. His brow was creased and his cheeks had turned crimson.

'I believe you are right, princess,' Ramble said, exchanging glances with her, Hogwash and Hokum. 'Though he would object to being a coward, downright denying past events is very unlike him.' He went over to the side of the bed, ignoring the king as he shrank back. The ghost spheres swarmed around him. That was when he saw it; indiscernible at any distance, but up close it was unmistakable. A purple shimmer surrounding the king's head; the curse that Princess Hurella had suspected. That was what the ghost spheres were attracted to, for not only did they swarm to people's emotions, but strong magic as well. And from what he could tell, this was far stronger than any he'd encountered within the past six hundred years.

'Your Majesty, you have been cursed,' he said calmly. 'I can break it for you, but you have to trust me. Please allow me to help you.'

'I will do no such th—'

'Father,' Princess Hurella said, raising her voice. 'You will do exactly as Ramble asks.'

The king eyed her coldly. 'I refuse.'

'Then I have no other choice. Ramble, please come with me to the crown jewels chamber and destroy them,' she said, returning her father's cold stare.

'No!' the king gasped. 'I'll do it, I'll do it,' he said, slouching back against his pillows in defeat.

Ramble looked at him and then at the princess, who gave a discreet wave of encouragement. He coughed, clearing his throat and raised his staff above the king, shaking the sleeves of his white robes back to his elbows.

'I call upon the strong winds, the gentle earth, the swift rivers and the light of both sun and moon. Help me free this man from the curse that clouds his mind and sends him into madness,' he said, controlling every syllable.

The runes on his staff glowed brightly and swirled around, and as they did so, the king began to glow too, the purple shimmer turning into ugly flames that flicked around him angrily. The king writhed in the bed, his eyes rolling back in his head so that only the whites showed. Princess Hurella clapped her hands to her mouth in horror as she watched him, but as fast as his convulsions had begun, they stopped.

The glow around the king turned bright like the runes on Ramble's staff, and then faded. The ghost spheres disappeared with it, leaving the king slumped over. Ramble lowered his staff, transforming it back into the small stick and tucking it inside his robes. He helped the king sit up, watching as his eyes focused on him. 'Goodness,' the king slurred. 'Is that really you, Ramble?'

'You know it's Ramble; he just rid you of your curse,' Princess Hurella said, staring at her father with incomprehension.

'Did he really? He always was helpful.'

Princess Hurella shot a glance a Ramble. He smiled. 'I think the curse has been on your father for quite some time,' he said, and then turned back to the king. 'Tell me, Your Majesty, what is the last thing you remember clearly?'

The king tugged at his chin. 'I believe it was when my nephew, Lord Tummet, visited. He lives near the Forest of Ainran and owns an inn there, the Everlasting Lantern, I think it's called. It was most unusual for him to travel so far to see me instead of sending a telegram, but he was quite anxious that I speak with him about a problem he's been having with the Walking Wolves.'

'And what exactly was the problem?' Ramble asked.

'I don't know. My memory goes all hazy after that, though I believe we had a nice coconut and cherry pancake over tea,' he said, licking his lips.

'That was seven months ago,' Princess Hurella said.

'Indeed?' Ramble said, raising an eyebrow at the king. 'Your nephew, Lord Tummet, did you say? He's not the one whose mother was a faun, is he?'

'Actually, he is,' the princess answered for her father. 'I used to laugh at him about it because one of his own legs is shaped like a goat's – though I realise now how unkind that was,' she added with a delicate cough. 'Do you know him, then?'

'Only from what His Majesty told me. But what concerns me is that he lives near the Forest of Ainran. If I remember rightly, then that's where Wilhelmina said her grandmother's wardrobe sometimes led to,' he said, exchanging glances with Hogwash and Hokum.

'Wardrobe? You're not talking about those silly old things my grandfather banned, are you?' the king said, laughing. 'I got stuck in one of them as a boy and scared the maids half to death because they thought I was a ghost. There was lots of room in it, though, and sometimes I caught glimpses of a forest, but I could never walk into it.' He looked at Ramble, and then at Hogwash and Hokum, who all had concerned expressions on their faces. 'Why have you all gone quiet?'

Ramble sighed. 'I suppose I'd better tell you what's happened again, seeing as you can't remember,' he said, pausing to take a breath. 'Your Majesty, I'm sorry to inform you that the Desrai are on the move. I don't know where they are yet, but they kidnapped a man from The Outside in order to lure me back to Treeshallow. I've sent one of my friends to investigate the mountains, where I know they fled to after the battle. I also have reason to believe that these magic wardrobes are involved somehow, but I need to look into it more to be certain.'

'The Desrai?' the king said, but unlike before, he didn't panic hysterically. Instead he shivered as though he'd caught a sudden chill, and looked up into Ramble's eyes. 'I knew that my lack of action after the battle would haunt me someday...but everyone was so happy, I just didn't want to think about the demons.'

His eyes grew watery as he spoke, but he sniffed and gave himself a shake. 'So, what do we do about it?'

'Well, we have two big questions: where are the demons hiding, and who put that curse on you and why?' Ramble replied.

Everyone stared at him. Who was powerful enough to break through the protective spells on the palace and carry out such a curse?'

18

DAMAGED WINGS

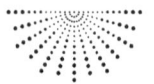

That evening, after politely refusing the king's offer to have them stay at the palace, Ramble, Hogwash and Hokum made their way back to 'The Dancing Donkey' to mull over everything they'd heard that day.

Ramble was exhausted, and sank gratefully into one of the common room's spacious armchairs. Though he hadn't realised at the time, the magic he'd used to free the king from his curse had been enormous, and had strained his body as much as if he'd spent a week doing physical labour.

'I'll be fine after food and a good night's rest. Don't worry,' he told the Earth Elves after they'd asked if he wanted them to fetch a healer. 'Tomorrow morning I'll be as—'

He was interrupted by the sound of hurried footsteps, and as he peered around the armchair's vast side, he saw the innkeeper running towards him, so flustered that her hair was hanging down in wild strands.

'Mr Ramble, sir,' she said, breathing heavily. 'I didn't know what to do; it's so awful. There's blood everywhere, I couldn't stop it.'

Both of Ramble's eyebrows shot up so far that they vanished into his hairline. 'What's the matter, is someone hurt?' he said, his gaze darting over to the serving tables, wondering if someone had accidentally sliced off a finger.

'It's your dragon, sir,' she said desperately as the rest of her hair tumbled down her shoulders in a big clump. 'He got back a few minutes ago, and his wings...his wings are...'

Ramble jumped to his feet. 'Where is he? Take me to him!'

She hurried from the room with Ramble right behind her and Hogwash and Hokum in close pursuit. Leading them out into the courtyard, she turned and made for the stables. As they got there, Ramble flung open the doors, readying himself for the worst.

Small was on the floor, and Lightfoot and Swiftwind were standing over him, touching his scaly skin with their glowing horns. Both of the little dragon's wings had large tears in them, and two great pools of blood surrounded him. Thanks to the unicorns' healing powers, the flow had lessened greatly.

Ramble sank to his knees in front of him. The dragon looked up and licked his face, but it didn't stop the tears from rolling down the wizard's cheeks. 'I'm so sorry, Small,' he said. 'I should never have sent you off on your own.'

Small made a forgiving whine, and nudged his head up against Ramble's robes. He lifted his wings, showing him that the bleeding had stopped completely now, but the wounds still looked so sore and terrible that it only made Ramble weep harder.

'Small's right,' Hokum said to him, putting a hand on his shoulder. 'You couldn't have known this would happen. None of us could.' She turned to the dragon and rubbed his head. 'How did this happen, Small?'

The dragon let out a series of grumbles and whines which Hokum listened to intently, her face growing more concerned by the minute. Finally, she rubbed his head again and turned back to the others.

'He made it to the mountains,' she said. 'There were lots of tracks in the snow, but at first he couldn't see anyone about. Then all of a sudden, a giant boulder was shot at him from somewhere and it went through one of his wings. He thinks he saw it come out of a trap door under the snow, but then another one hit him and he didn't see where it came from. He only made it back because there was a dragon clan passing nearby. Two of them volunteered to carry him back, and they're waiting to speak to you at the north gate of the city.'

'Alright, I'll go and meet with them now. I'll need you with me to translate, Hokum.' He turned to her brother and the innkeeper (who was staring in awe at the unicorns). 'Hogwash, please get him something hot to eat and drink, and if you can find a healer, ask them to come at once. He needs a poultice made from a mix of Kingsfoil and grape vine, bound with a cloth made of pure, un-dyed silk. I'll be back as soon as I can,' he said, spurring into action. 'Oh, and give Lightfoot and Swiftwind something nice to eat too; if it wasn't for them, Small might have bled to death.'

'I know just what they'll like,' Hogwash said, and then questioned the innkeeper about where the nearest healer was, watching the wizard and Hokum sprint out of the door.

The north gate wasn't far from the inn. After five minutes they reached it, panting as they passed the guards on either side. They stepped out of the city and looked around, spotting two large boulders resting on the grass in front of them.

They walked up to them and bowed low, catching their breath.

'I am Wizard Ramble,' he said, keeping his eyes firmly in line with the middle of the boulders. 'I thank you for rescuing my friend.'

There was a low rumbling as the two boulders started moving, growing long necks and arms and sprouting wings. They were no longer boulders, but two large, rock coloured dragons. They towered over him, almost the size of a house.

One of them began to speak, making the same grumbling and whining sounds as Small had made. Not for the first time, Ramble cursed himself for never learning to speak dragon language.

Hokum listened to the dragon closely. 'She says her name is Muldred,' she translated to Ramble. 'Head of the Rock Dragon Clan. The one next to her is her son, Ilmar.'

'I am honoured to meet you, Lady Muldred. And you also, Ilmar,' Ramble said, nodding his head to the great dragons.

They inclined their heads back to him and then Muldred began to speak once more. Again, Hokum listened to her, nodding here and there, before translating back to Ramble.

'They saw what happened to Small. He was indeed hit by a large boulder coming from a trapdoor in the snow. The second boulder, however, came from a small group of demons who snuck out from the side of a mountain when he was looking away. They say the demons retreated as soon as he started falling to the ground. She and her son caught him in mid-air and carried him back here,' she said, pausing to listen some more as the dragon carried on talking.

She let out a small gasp of surprise. 'She says that this wasn't the first attack on a dragon who has passed over the mountains. Several months ago, two of their own flew off to gather materials for their nests, but only one came back.'

At this point, the other dragon stepped forwards and began speaking. Hokum nodded to him and continued. 'It was Ilmar and one of his friends, but only he returned. They were attacked with boulders too, and his friend got hit, but there was a snowstorm there at the time and Ilmar couldn't rescue him. When he went back with the rest of the clan, they found no sign of him.'

Ramble cursed, using words that his mother would have grounded him for had she heard. 'So, not only have the Desrai kidnapped Mr Rogers, but now they appear to have captured a dragon, too. This is bad. Very, very bad.'

The two dragons eyed him with concern. Ramble looked back at them, knowing that it would do no good to keep anything from them. 'Dragons such as yourselves have long been revered as the most powerful and wise creatures in all of Treeshallow. Because of that, it has long been forbidden to kill one of your kind, but that is not the only reason. The other, and perhaps even more serious reason, is that dragon blood is the only known substance that can break through protective spells, such as those used to repel curses. To do so, it has to be refined to a powder first, using a technique that only a very strong wizard or mage will know. As it happens, we know that the protective spells at the palace were overridden, because I've just broken a curse that was put on the king around seven months ago.'

Both Muldred and Ilmar let out a loud howl at this, with sparks shooting from their nostrils, and began speaking rapidly. Hokum listened to them sadly. 'They say that seven months would be close to when Ilmar's friend disappeared.'

'It's as I thought, then. I believe the demons may have used your friend's blood to place a curse on the king,' he said, holding up his hands as they let out another howl. 'There's no need to panic. Only an ounce of powdered dragon blood would have been needed to break the protective spells, so there's every chance that he's still alive and imprisoned somewhere, along with a human from The Outside.'

No sooner had he finished speaking did the dragons open their wings in preparation to take off.

'Wait,' Ramble said to them. 'If you try to go after him now, then the demons may try to capture you as well. I have someone I want to rescue too, but I can't even attempt to do so without a plan. Please, trust me. I intend to fight the demons and get both of our friends back safely.'

Ilmar snorted two great plumes of smoke and growled, but Muldred growled back at him and folded her wings. She said something quickly to Hokum.

'Muldred wants to trust you, but she's not convinced you can defeat the demons again by yourself. She knows you pushed yourself too hard last time, and also fears that the demons may have prepared something to cancel out the spell you used if you try it again,' she explained, but Ramble smiled.

'That's why I'm not planning on fighting them by myself again,' he replied, looking directly at the dragons. They stared back at him, but made no sound. 'Will you trust me?'

Muldred let out a low grumble in reply and lowered her head in a bow; a dragon's show of acceptance. Then she and Ilmar took off, soaring up into the sky and out of sight.

19

LINKING THE CHAIN

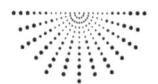

'Wizard Ramble?'

Ramble woke up in bed, staring around the room in an effort to make out who was speaking to him in the darkness. He could hear Hogwash and Hokum breathing deeply in their sleep, and Small, feeling much better, had taken up his usual place above Ramble's pillow.

He blinked, wondering if he had dreamt it, but the voice came again.

'Wizard Ramble? Can you hear me?'

The voice was very familiar and, as there was no one else in the room, there was only one person it could be. 'Wilhelmina, is that you?' he whispered.

'Yes. You weren't asleep, were you?' she asked, he voice sounding anxious.

'Never mind that,' he said, stretching and pulling back the covers. 'Only something important would make you contact me this early in the morning. What is it?'

He grimaced as he put his feet on the cold floor, wriggling his toes before going over to the window. There was a pale light coming through the gap in the heavy curtains, and he pushed them apart to see the sun beginning to rise.

'It's about those wardrobes you told me about,' Wilhelmina said, taking a breath. 'I was talking to the Dwarves of Neves earlier, and I asked to have a look at the field where the wardrobes are buried to see if any had been dug up. They're experts on digging, so I thought that even if the demons managed it years ago, the dwarves would still find traces of the ground being disturbed.'

'Go on,' Ramble said, his attention sparked.

'Well, they just came back. It seems that the ground was loose in two places. One of the wardrobes is missing completely, but the other is still there. The strange thing is, it was reburied in a different position, so that the doors are facing up. They found it close to the surface, and the doors were only covered with leaves, not earth.'

Ramble's eyes narrowed. 'Almost like a trap door in the ground?' he asked.

'Yes, actually,' Wilhelmina replied, sounding surprised. 'That's the same conclusion that the dwarves came up with.'

'Did they happen to go inside the wardrobe at all?' he asked.

'They did. It was one of the faulty ones, though. Do you remember I told you about the one my grandmother had? That sometimes led to the Forest of Ainran?'

Ramble's eyes narrowed even more. 'Does this one happen to lead to a forest too, by any chance?' he said.

'How did you know that?' she asked.

'Just a hunch,' he said. 'Is it the same forest?'

'The dwarves seem to think so. They recognised some of the trees there, which only grow in Ainran. The connection is very strong in this particular wardrobe though, not like the one my grandmother had. They tried it a handful of times, and could pass back and forth easily every time,' she said.

'Like the Door Between Worlds connects Treeshallow to the Outside,' he mused, his mind forming deep suspicions of everything they had found out so far. An image came into his mind from when he had come through the Door Between Worlds and ended up in the field. There had been a large puddle there absolutely filled with ghost spheres.

'Wilhelmina, did the dwarves notice if the leaves covering the wardrobe were wet, as though there'd been a puddle there recently?'

'Yes, part of it was still there. When they opened the doors, it all dripped down into the room within and came out into the forest. Why do you ask?' she said, her voice strong with curiosity.

'Because I saw a giant puddle the day I came back to Treeshallow, and above it were hundreds and hundreds of ghost spheres. They must have been attracted to the wardrobe's magic, and if they were, then it means that someone used it recently.' He scratched his chin, thinking everything over.

Seven months ago, the king fell under a curse when his nephew, Lord Tummet, visited from the Forest of Ainran, and around the same time, a rock dragon was mysteriously attacked in the mountains. Then a fortnight ago, the demons went through the Door Between Worlds and kidnapped Mr Rogers, somehow remaining hidden from the rest of Treeshallow, and then the goblins were forced out of their homes by the Underons, who in turn had been made to flee from theirs. And now Wilhelmina had discovered that two of the magic wardrobes had been moved, one missing completely, and one reburied to act as a trap door to the Forest of Ainran.

'You've figured out something, haven't you?' she asked quietly.

'Perhaps,' he said. 'But I think I may have to pay a visit to someone first. If I'm right, then this could very well end up in a battle after all. Small was attacked in the mountains yesterday, but was rescued by the Rock Dragon Clan. They told me that one of their own went missing there. I promised to rescue him along with Mr Rogers, but I can't act alone. If I give you the call, will you help me?'

'You know I will, but I'm only a simple witch. There's nothing I can do against the demons that you can't,' she said doubtfully.

'You can raise an army for me,' he replied, smiling.

'An army? Made up of who?' she spluttered.

'I'm sure you'll come up with a few people. But don't panic, it might not come to that,' he said, truly hoping that it wouldn't.

The sun came up fully and shone into the room, making everyone else stir. Hogwash and Hokum woke up to find that Ramble was already dressed and waiting for them, rubbing Small's stomach and watching the dragon wag his tail.

'You're up early,' Hokum said, climbing down her Goldus tree and going behind the changing screen to change out of her night-clothes and into her dress.

'There's something important I have to do today, but I've got to see the king first,' he said. 'We...might be leaving the city.'

She stepped out from the changing screen, one eyebrow raised. Hogwash poked his head out from under a leafy branch and looked at him with a similar expression, but Ramble shook his head.

'I'll explain it to you along with the king. If we leave soon, we should just catch him at breakfast,' he said.

The Earth Elves knew it would do no good to argue, so instead they got ready and followed him and Small down the stairs into the inn's common room. Saying a quick greeting to the innkeeper, they marched out the door and made their way straight to the palace.

They reached the large staircase leading up to the main palace doors, and in his haste, Ramble almost flew up them, leaving Hogwash, Hokum and Small doing their best to keep up. When they got to the large double doors, the guards either side let them through to the entrance hall beyond, where another guard was waiting to enquire about their business.

'We're here to speak with the king,' Ramble said to him. 'I was hoping to catch him at breakfast before his official duties began.'

'Is the matter urgent? His Majesty usually turns away early visitors,' the guard asked.

'It is,' Ramble said, so seriously that the guard felt stupid for even considering that it wasn't.

'I'll announce you right away, then, Your Wizardship,' he said, and scurried out of the room. A few minutes passed before he came back, slightly out of breath. 'The king will see you.'

He led them to the dining hall, opening the door and standing aside to let them pass. The king and Princess Hurella were both seated at a large, oval shaped table, filled with so much food that it could easily have fed a company of thirty. The king had his face buried in the remains of a cream cake as they entered, so it was Princess Hurella who spoke to them first. She hadn't missed their eyes scanning the full table.

'My father is a fussy eater. He can never decide what he wants, so the chefs always send up a selection. Please, have a seat. I'm sure you've all skipped your own breakfasts to get here this early, so you're welcome to share ours,' she said, gesturing to the table. The king mumbled in agreement, his mouth too full of cake to say anything coherent.

Small took up the offer immediately and bounded up to sit on one of the seats, tucking into a large plate of Bubock root sausages and porridge. Everyone laughed except for Ramble, who had taken a seat next to the king, ignoring his hunger for the time being.

'I received some information from Wilhelmina the Witch this morning,' he said, getting straight to the point. 'Those wardrobes I mentioned yesterday, buried near the Door Between Worlds, have been disturbed. Two of them have been dug up and moved, though one of them was reburied with its doors facing up. I believe it's being used as a trap door. And yesterday, Small was attacked when he was in the mountains with two large boulders, one of which came from such a door.'

Princess Hurella dropped her cutlery and leapt up to examine Small. When she saw the large holes in his wings, she rounded on Ramble angrily. 'How could you have let this happen?'

'I made a mistake,' Ramble replied, the remorse in his eyes so evident that the princess's gaze softened a little. 'It never occurred to me that someone would attack him while he was in the air.'

Small looked at him and whined, leaning over to lick his hand. Ramble sighed and rubbed the dragon's scaly head.

'So you believe that there is a connection between the reburied wardrobe and this trap door in the mountains?' the king asked, after a moment.

'Yes, but not directly. The wardrobe that was reburied led to the Forest of Ainran, not to the mountains. Wilhelmina had the Dwarves of Neves test it before she told me,' he said.

'Then how are these situations linked?' the king said, rubbing his brow.

'I can't be certain, but I believe that the second wardrobe which was dug up is being used as the trap door in the mountains,' Ramble replied. 'I've only heard rumours of the wardrobes leading to the Forest of Ainran, never to anywhere else, so I have a strong feeling that the one buried in the mountains also leads there.'

'What does that mean, then?' the king said, starting on another cake.

'It means that I'm going to have a long talk with your nephew, Lord Tummet.'

20

LORD TUMMET

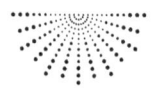

The Forest of Ainran was north of the Royal City, and the road was steep and uneven. The carriage, pulled by Lightfoot and Swiftwind, rocked back and forth as they cantered forwards as fast as they could manage.

'We're not pushing them too hard, are we?' Ramble asked Hogwash, as he poked his head out of the window and saw the sweat on the unicorns' backs. They were going at such a speed that his cheeks flapped about in the wind.

'Absolutely not,' Hogwash said with a laugh, steering them around a bend in the road. 'Unicorns have much more endurance than horses or even pegasi have. You should know that.'

'I do know that,' Ramble replied as the carriage crashed through a puddle. A splatter of mud caught him in the face and he brushed it away, spitting out the grit that had landed in his mouth. 'It just feels like we're going awfully fast,' he said, pulling a face.

'We are,' Hogwash said. 'You told me to get us there as quickly as possible, and that's exactly what I'm doing.' He shook his head and muttered something under his breath that Ramble couldn't quite hear.

Ramble took a deep breath and retreated back into the carriage. Hokum looked up from the map that Princess Hurella had given her and let out a giggle.

'You look like a schoolboy who's been up to no good,' she said, taking a handkerchief from her pocket and wiping away the mud that he'd missed.

'I am a schoolboy...well, I *was*, before all this happened. I feel like I've aged ten years,' he said, and she laughed even more. 'What's so funny?'

'Well, you *have* aged ten years,' she said. 'Your body went from being ten years old to twenty the moment you stepped through the Door Between Worlds. Ramble may have been around for hundreds of years, but he's always had the appearance of a twenty-year-old.'

'Even though I know that's true, it still gives me a headache to think about it,' he said, narrowing his eyes. 'Anyway, when will we reach the forest?'

'If we carry on at this speed, we should get there in two more days,' she replied, showing him their location on the map. They were exactly halfway between the Royal City and the Forest of Ainran.

'Good. We should make it in time, then,' he said.

'Make it in time? What do you mean?' she asked, looking him at him directly.

'I think Lord Tummet is working with the demons, and either has a mage on his side, or is secretly one himself. He may very well be harbouring them while they prepare to attack.'

Hokum went cold. 'Then we could be riding right into their clutches?'

'Perhaps,' he replied. 'But that all depends on who's really running things. If Lord Tummet is the one controlling the demons, then we might be in trouble. If it's the other way around, though, and Lord Tummet is actually under their control, then we might be okay.'

'How did you work that out?' she asked, avoiding Small's tail as he flicked it near her in his sleep.

'If he's under their control, then it's unlikely that the demons are actually nearby, so if Tummet threatens to go to them we can call his bluff and overpower him.'

'You seem very sure of yourself,' she said with a smirk.

'That's because I am. I might ramble on a lot, but I do give my plans a lot of thought,' he said, grinning back at her.

Another two days of travel passed as Hokum had said it would, and as the moon began to rise that night, Hogwash stopped the carriage in front of a large building looming up in the darkness. A tall, black lantern stood outside it, lit with a flame that changed colour with every flicker. The Everlasting Lantern Inn.

The inn itself was lit by a multitude of smaller lanterns, containing normal flames that provided plenty of light from the surrounding gloom. Ramble, Hokum and Small got out of the carriage as Hogwash jumped down from the driving seat, rubbing his numb backside.

'It's bigger than I remember it,' he remarked, climbing up onto Lightfoot and Swiftwind's harnesses so that he could loosen them to make the unicorns more comfortable. They were panting heavily; staring at a trough in front of them that was completely empty.

Ramble tapped his staff against it, and it filled up instantly with cool, fresh water. They drank from it thirstily. 'You've been here before?' he asked, turning to Hogwash.

'Yes,' Hokum said, answering for her brother as he jumped down from the harnesses. 'Our parents brought us to visit our cousins. They live close to here. We didn't stay at the inn though, not with so many trees around that we could sleep in.

'So what did it look like back then?' Ramble asked, as they made their way to the entrance.

'It was just a shack, I think, with only three rooms. But that was before Lord Tummet's late father took it over and tried to make it a tourist spot,' she replied.

'And it has had great success ever since,' someone said, opening the door with a bang. A slender man stood in the doorway, with at least six scarves around his neck, each a different colour. He had pointed ears and a goatee, and, though he was obviously trying to hide it by wearing trousers, they spotted a cloven hoof where his right foot should have been. The leg of a goat; inherited by his faun mother. Just like Princess Hurella had told them.

He smiled and stood to aside, waving them in with a slight bow. 'Please come in, we have plenty of rooms available,' he said, speaking with a slight lisp. He shut the door behind them and limped over; it was painfully obvious to everyone that his goat leg was considerably smaller than his human one.

'You are Lord Tummet, are you not?' Ramble asked, forcing his gaze away.

'Indeed I am. Who do I have the pleasure of meeting, if I may ask?' he said, his lisp even stronger than before.

'My name is Wizard Ramble. I'm afraid I've come here on official business for your uncle, King Albrand of Treeshallow.'

'Goodness!' Lord Tummet exclaimed, unable to disguise the flash of fear that crossed his face. 'What kind of business is it that would make the king send someone all the way out here?'

'There was a problem with the palace security some months ago,' Ramble said, keeping the conversation light. He couldn't let Lord Tummet know that they were on to him until they'd established who was working for who. 'The protective spells were broken somehow.'

'But my uncle and my dear cousin Hurella are safe, are they not?' Lord Tummet asked.

'They are now, yes. I've repaired and strengthened all the spells so that they're working properly again,' Ramble replied, telling the truth. 'But I'm afraid a strong curse was put on your uncle, one that made him so irrational with fear that he locked himself in his rooms. There is only one thing that can break a spell cast against curses. Do you know what it is?'

'Me? Why would I? I have no experience with magic at all,' Lord Tummet replied timidly, licking his dry lips.

'It's dragon blood,' Ramble told him. 'And it's the reason why the king sent me here. Owning such a popular inn, he thought you would meet all sorts of people, perhaps even some with...questionable habits. Have you ever heard someone mention dragon blood?'

'I should think not! What sort of business do you think I have here? And who would be able to get their hands on it anyway? And for what reason? he questioned, his voice getting higher with every word as his eyes darted back and forth between them. 'Procuring dragon blood would mean injuring a dragon at the very least, and I have no customers who would even dream of doing such a thing.'

'What about you? Would you dream of it?' Ramble asked, his eyes going cold as he looked Lord Tummet full in the face. Behind him, Hogwash and Hokum snuck off discreetly into the kitchen.

'Of course not,' Lord Tummet replied, swallowing. Ramble noticed that there were beads of sweat appearing on his brow.

'I don't think you're telling the truth, Lord Tummet,' Ramble said, seeing the two Earth Elves reappear again from the kitchen 'In fact, I think you were keeping dragon blood in your kitchen cupboards.'

Lord Tummet's eyes fell on Hogwash and Hokum too, and his mouth dropped open in horror. Hokum was holding a large jar full of red powder. On its label, in neat, slanted handwriting, were the words 'Dragon Blood'.

21

FULL BARRELS

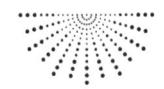

'I have no idea where you got that,' Lord Tummet said desperately. 'I've never seen that jar before in my life.'

'It's no use, Lord Tummet,' Ramble said calmly. 'We know that you were visiting the king at the time the curse was put on him. He remembered your meeting clearly, and the only way to break through the protective spells at the palace is to sprinkle dragon blood around. Only someone who is versed in magic can turn dragon blood into a powder. Was it you, or did someone else do it?' he demanded, watching Lord Tummet's mouth quiver.

'I...I did it. My father was something of a mage; he used to teach me as a boy. Many of the guests who stay here come for our healing treatments,' Lord Tummet replied, hunkering down under Ramble's accusing gaze.

'If you normally use your powers to heal people, then why would you go against that and curse someone, especially you own uncle?'

'It wasn't my fault. They were threatening me,' Lord Tummet whimpered, sniffing thickly. 'If I hadn't have done it, then they would have burnt down my inn.'

'And who exactly are *they?*' Ramble asked, knowing full well who he meant.

'The...the demons,' Lord Tummet said, shivering as he spoke. 'They showed up about a year or so after the battle, but there were only a handful of them back then. Sometimes they would vanish from sight, only to come back days later. They left us alone for years, so it didn't bother me much, but then father went to collect firewood one day and never came back. I thought that maybe he'd caught his foot somewhere and was unable to walk, but when I went out looking for him, I found the demons. They were...'

He made a gagging sound, as though he were about to be sick. Ramble quickly fetched a chair and sat him down. Lord Tummet wiped his brow with the tip of one of his scarves and took some deep breaths.

'Do you know how demons breed?' he said, staring at Ramble. His voice was soft and somehow distant.

'No,' Ramble confessed. 'But I know it's not a simple as the males and females pairing up together.'

Lord Tummet let out a shaky laugh. 'Demons aren't male or female,' he said, swallowing. 'The way they breed...is by capturing and eating large animals, particularly magical ones. It makes them sort of...split in half, I suppose, becoming two demons instead of one.' He paused, his body shaking so violently that for a moment Ramble thought he was having a seizure. It subsided just enough for him to speak. 'That's why they were there when I went looking for father. They were...eating him.'

Hokum gasped and dropped the jar of dragon blood, but luckily Hogwash caught it before it hit the floor. Everyone was silent, staring at Lord Tummet in absolute horror. Even Small was shaken, letting out a low whine.

'And the demons really grew in number by..?' Ramble murmured. The idea was so horrendous that he couldn't bring himself to say it.

'Yes. There were only thirteen or so, but then they grew to twenty-six,' Lord Tummet said, before turning to Hogwash and

Hokum. 'There used to be Earth Elves like you living in this forest, but they all vanished last year, and the demons grew to several hundred in a matter of weeks. I didn't think that they would go after them because your people are so small and unobtrusive, but I suppose your magic was too tempting to them.'

'No...no, that can't be! They couldn't have, they just couldn't have!' Hokum cried, sinking to the floor. Hogwash put his arm around her and glowered at Lord Tummet with burning eyes.

'Why didn't you tell someone that the demons had spread here when they first arrived?' he spat. 'If there were so few, then the king could have easily got rid of them! Because of you, our cousins are dead!'

A lump formed in Ramble's throat as he looked on, unable to do anything to comfort them. 'Tell me,' he said to Lord Tummet, who was also in tears. 'Why did the demons want to curse the king?'

'Isn't it obvious? If the king was too afraid to do anything, then all the demons would have to do to take over Treeshallow would be to defeat you. That's what they want; to defeat you like you defeated them. They know that without the king's army, it'll be left up to you. They want it to be like last time, only now it'll be on their terms,' Lord Tummet answered.

'What do you mean?' Ramble said.

'They've come up with a way to defend themselves against fire to stop you using the same spell again. I don't know the details, so please don't ask me. The only part of their plan I knew about was kidnapping the old man from The Outside and capturing a dragon so I could use its blood to break the protective spells on the palace.'

'You know about Mr Rogers? And the rock dragon?' Ramble asked.

'I do,' Lord Tummet said quietly.

'Well, where are they?' Ramble said impatiently.

'They're in a wardrobe,' he replied, straightening himself in the chair. 'I suppose you know that the demons dug them up again.'

'They've got two, haven't they?' Ramble said. 'One buried by the

Door Between Worlds, and one in the mountains. They both lead back here, if I'm correct.'

'Perhaps you *are* as smart as I've heard,' Lord Tummet said, giving Ramble a thin smile. 'I don't know which wardrobe they're in, but I can show you the place where the demons appear in the woods after they've come through one. It might make you too late, however...'

'Too late? For what? What is it you're hiding, Lord Tummet?' Hogwash snapped angrily, wiping away the residue of his tears. Hokum was still crying silently by his side, but the glare she gave Lord Tummet was full of hate. Small, sensing their discontent, ambled up to Lord Tummet and snorted a large flame from his nostrils. Lord Tummet shrank back from him, almost toppling off the chair.

'The demons aren't here anymore,' he squeaked, his eyes locked on Small's smoking nostrils. 'They've already left for the Royal City. They plan to attack it from within.

'How? As soon as someone sees them, they'll alert the king, and now that the curse is broken he'll be ready to take action,' Ramble said.

Lord Tummet laughed sadly. 'No one will see them. They're hidden in barrels being transported by merchants, who think they're full of food for the harvest festival next week. The guards at the city gates won't even suspect them.'

Ramble's eyes widened. He took hold of Lord Tummet's many scarves and pulled him out of the chair towards the door. 'Take me to where Mr Rogers and the rock dragon are,' he said, and then turned to Small, Hogwash and Hokum. 'You can all wait in the carriage. I'll be alright by myself.'

Hogwash started to protest, but Ramble held up his hand and marched out the door, dragging Lord Tummet along behind him.

The sky was inky black around them, and the air was cold. As they moved away from the lanterns surrounding the inn, Ramble took out the stick from his robes and turned it into his staff. 'Light,' he whispered, and a bright glowing ball shot up into the air, floating along beside them as they walked. Its light shone through the trees, allowing Lord Tummet to find the path through them that he needed.

Low branches speared out everywhere, making them duck frequently, and every now and then they heard the howling of a Walking Wolf nearby. Lord Tummet whimpered whenever he heard them, but Ramble forced him to keep going.

'Relax. Walking Wolves only hurt humans if they're hurt themselves; there's nothing to worry about,' he said after the fifth time, hoping he was right. If Lord Tummet was lying or some of the demons had stayed behind to guard the entrance to the wardrobes, then there would be something to worry about.

Twenty minutes passed, and they came to a large tree with a trunk the width of a small elephant. Despite its size, it was very spindly and had smooth, knobbly bark.

'I've never seen a tree like this,' Ramble said, gazing up at it.

'Then you can't have been to this forest before. This is an Ainran tree, which the forest gets its name from. They used to grow all around here, but now there are only a few left. Most of them were used to make those magic wardrobes. I think that's why they lead out to this tree,' Lord Tummet replied, still with his scarves held tightly by Ramble.

'So the way into the wardrobes is somewhere here, then?'

The half-faun nodded. 'One comes out this side of the tree, the other comes out behind it. All you've got to do to get in is walk towards the tree.'

Ramble eyed at him suspiciously, but did as he said. He got to a few inches away and then found himself in a large, black room. He looked around and, lying chained up on the floor, was a rock dragon as big as Muldred and Ilmar had been. Next to him, appearing terribly small in comparison, was Mr Rogers.

22

CHAINS AND SCARVES

Ramble rushed over, placing his staff on the chains binding them together, and commanded the restraints to break. Each link cracked down the middle and the whole lot fell to the floor.

He put his hands on Mr Rogers's shoulder and sat him up against the rock dragon's back. Mr Rogers blinked, blinded by the floating light hovering at Ramble's shoulder. He looked tired and thin, and there were deep cuts on his hands and face.

As his eyes began to focus, he managed a weary smile. 'So you finally found me,' he said hoarsely.

'I'm sorry it took so long. If I'd have noticed the wardrobes earlier...' Ramble replied, but Mr Rogers shook his head.

'It's not your fault; I knew full well what I was throwing you into. I suspect it took nearly this long to get your memories back, yes?'

'Yes,' he said. It was hard to look at the old man knowing now that he used to be Ramble. 'Isn't it strange for you?'

Mr Rogers chuckled softly. 'It is, but I knew the instant I transferred my powers to you as an infant that we would one day meet like this.' He stood up on shaky legs and wobbled violently. Ramble grabbed him by the arm to support him, glancing around for something the old man could use as a walking stick.

A small twig was stuck to his shoes from his trek through the forest. He picked it up turned it into a knobbly cane.

'Not bad,' Mr Rogers grinned. 'Not a masterpiece, perhaps, but good enough for support.'

'I'm glad you like it,' Ramble said wryly. 'Now, let me check our scaly friend here,' he said, looking at the dragon. It still hadn't stirred, and its breath was shallow.

'He's very weak. Been here for months, I think.'

'Seven months,' Ramble said, turning sharply to Lord Tummet, who had been trying to edge back out of the wardrobe. Ramble held up his staff and whispered a few words, making the half-faun's many scarves stick to the floor. He whimpered. 'That's correct, isn't it?' Ramble continued.

Lord Tummet inclined his head slightly, careful not to meet the wizard's eyes.

'Well, that would explain the poor creature's condition. Why did they capture him, Ramble? You didn't look surprised to see him, so I assume you know,' Mr Rogers said.

'They used his blood to break the protective spells at the palace so they could curse the king,' Ramble replied, examining at the dragon's head. It was almost as large as he was, a fact that would have been terrifying if the dragons of Treeshallow weren't known to hunt only for what they needed and never attacked without being provoked.

The dragon's large eyes were closed, and two streaks of crusted tears ran down his gaunt cheeks. Ramble touched him lightly on his broad forehead. The dragon's eyes opened slowly and locked onto him, the fear in them only too obvious.

'Don't be afraid, it's alright now,' Ramble whispered soothingly, inspecting him for injuries. One of his front toes was missing, cut off at the knuckle, not even leaving a stump. The wound looked dry and sore, but at least it wasn't bleeding. There was also a hole in one of his wings, just like the ones Small had, but the skin around it was almost fully healed.

'I'm afraid we've got to get out of here,' Ramble said calmly. 'The demons are on their way to the Royal City, and I've got to hurry so I can stop them before they get there. Can you stand?'

The dragon lifted his head with difficulty, but managed to push himself up to standing, towering over them. He stretched out his wings, filling most of the room, before folding them back down. Suddenly Ramble had an idea. 'Muldred and your friend Ilmar are waiting for your return. I can't fix your wing completely, but I might be able to temporarily allow you to fly,' he said, glancing at the hole. Then he looked at Mr Rogers, his eyes moving down to the sporran on the old man's kilt. 'I'm going to need that,' he said.

Mr Rogers took it off and handed it to him, one eyebrow raised with interest. Ramble inspected it closely before moving on to measure the hole in the dragon's wing, using his staff for reference. Satisfied with his calculations, he picked the sporran apart so that it was one flat piece of leather. Then he made it grow as large as the hole, fitting it over the top and sticking it there with magic. The dragon looked at his wing in surprise and gave it a few flaps, making a great gust of wind in the otherwise still room. Seeing this, he unfolded his other wing and flapped them both, hovering a little above the ground.

'Think it's good enough to fly properly with?' Ramble asked.

The dragon gave an enthusiastic grunt and leapt through the wardrobe doors into the Forest of Ainran. Ramble and Mr Rogers followed quickly behind, dragging Lord Tummet along with them.

As they stepped out onto the forest floor, the dragon stopped abruptly, staring at the half-faun with a low growl. Lord Tummet took a few steps backs, tripping over a tree root and falling to the ground. The dragon lowered its head to him, sniffing at his scarves. Its eyes narrowed and a huge burst of smoke erupted from its nostrils, sending him into a coughing fit.

'If I'm not mistaken,' Ramble said dryly, 'I believe he can smell his blood on you. I don't think he's too happy about it. Perhaps you should apologise.'

Lord Tummet gulped and pawed at the ground with his cloven hoof, resisting the urge to back away to the nearest tree. 'I'm sorry, Mr Dragon,' he said, a noticeable quiver in his voice. 'I didn't want the demons to hurt you, or to use your blood, but I was too afraid to help you and the old man. I thought they would kill me if I tried.'

Mr Rogers scoffed as the dragon let out another blast of smoke. 'I wouldn't be satisfied with an apology like that, either,' he said, patting the dragon's great neck. 'Unfortunately, we have to hurry, so there's no time for a better one.'

The dragon looked at him gravely and turned to Ramble, who was waiting quietly beside them. 'When you find your clan, I need you to ask them for a favour,' he began. 'As soon as they can, I need them to make contact with a witch called Wilhelmina over in the town near the Door Between Worlds. I'll tell her that you're coming so that it'll be easy to find her. She'll explain everything from there on. Will you do so?'

The dragon nodded and Ramble sighed with relief. He waved goodbye and watched as the dragon beat his large wings, taking off into the air and soaring out of sight as though his wing had never been damaged at all.

'So, then,' Mr Rogers said, leaning heavily on his walking stick and turning to Ramble with interest. 'What do we do from here?'

Ramble smiled at him. He was already starting to sound like his old self. 'Well, first we had better get back to the carriage. Lightfoot and Swiftwind should be able to restore some of your energy, and our good friend here is sure to have some food lying around in his kitchen that we can take with us,' he replied, indicating Lord Tummet. Ramble offered Tummet a hand so that the half-faun could pull himself up off the floor, and then pushed him to the front so he could lead the way back to the Everlasting Lantern Inn.

Lord Tummet gave them no time to bully him further, speeding off through the trees without even looking back to see if they were following. Unfortunately, he ran through a thick set of branches and his scarves caught in them tightly. He struggled, but was unable to break free.

'Now that's what you get for letting a poor old man hobble along behind you,' Mr Rogers said, as he and Ramble caught up to him.

Ramble rolled his eyes and touched the branches with his staff. The scarves fell free and fluttered to Lord Tummet's side, allowing him to move again. He gave the half-faun a withering look. Lord Tummet swallowed and gingerly made his way to the inn, making sure not to leave them behind this time.

23
PREPARATIONS

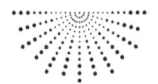

As they reached the carriage, they found Hogwash and Small waiting for them with several large bags of food, having already raided Lord Tummet's kitchen. Hokum was inside it, trying to get some rest to relieve the shock of losing their cousins.

'Who's this old man?' Hogwash asked when he saw Mr Rogers.

'I can see you haven't changed over the years,' Mr Rogers answered. 'Still, I suppose that's a good thing, given the circumstances.'

Hogwash's eyes widened. 'So *you're* Mr Rogers?' he said, breaking into a grin.

'You mean you don't recognise him?' Ramble asked, surprised.

'Why would I?' Hogwash said. 'When he was Ramble, he looked just like you do. How could I possibly recognise him from that?'

Ramble looked at Mr Rogers, who was being watched closely by Small. Hogwash had a point; they looked nothing alike. 'It's alright, Small, he's a friend,' he said.

The little dragon walked over to Mr Rogers slowly and put his nose in his hand. He sniffed, but then jumped back, glancing wildly between him and Ramble. 'What's the matter?' Ramble asked.

'I must still have the scent of your magic on me. I thought after ten years it would have left my body completely, but it seems not,' Mr Rogers replied, coaxing Small back to him. 'He'll understand soon, I'm sure.'

He walked over to Lightfoot and Swiftwind, who reacted the same way. Ramble reassured them, and they let Mr Rogers stand in front of them so they could heal him.

They rested their horns on his shoulders, their glow intensifying and covering him completely. Slowly, the cuts and scratches on his face and arms closed up and he was able to regain his balance. Then the glow faded and they moved away, taking a long drink from the trough.

'Thank you, my friends,' he said, patting their necks. 'I feel better than I have done in days.'

'That's not surprising,' Hogwash said, opening the carriage door and heaving the large bag of food inside with a grunt. 'Nothing can beat a unicorn for healing, and you had *two* healing you.'

Mr Rogers gave him a wry smile. 'There's no need to tell me that. I may not be Ramble anymore, but my memory of that time is just fine.'

'Oh? I thought people started to lose their memories when they reached their senior years,' Hogwash replied, keeping a straight face.

Before Mr Rogers could reply, Ramble broke in. 'We should get going. There'll be plenty of time to talk later, but for now we need to move, otherwise we'll be too late to stop the demons from entering the city. I don't know if we'll make it as it is.'

Mr Rogers climbed into the carriage with Small, sitting next to Hokum, who was motionless in her sleep, while Hogwash jumped up into the driver's seat. Ramble looked at Lord Tummet, deciding what to do with him. He could leave him there, but what if Tummet managed to get a message to the demons and alert them to Ramble's plans? No, it wouldn't do; it was too risky.

Grabbing Tummet by the scarves again, he pulled the half-faun into the carriage with him. Settled, Hogwash took up the reins and led them off into the night.

Hokum woke up as the sun began to rise and looked at everyone in great surprise. With three grown men, a dragon, herself and five bags of food, the carriage had become rather cramped.

'How are you feeling now?' Ramble asked her quietly, trying to move his legs into a more comfortable position and failing.

'I'm alright,' she said, attempting a smile. 'I just want to stop the demons before they hurt anyone else.'

He put a hand on her shoulder. 'We will. I promise that we will,' he said, trying to convince himself as much as her. He put his staff to his forehead, managing to avoid hitting anyone with the other end, and pictured Wilhelmina firmly in his mind. 'Contact Locate,' he muttered, hoping the witch was up to the task he was about to give her.

'Ramble, is that you?' her voice sounded loudly in his ears.

'I'm afraid so, Wilhelmina. I didn't want to ask this of you, but I really do need your help.'

'You want me to raise an army for you, like you said before?' she asked.

'Yes. I have no choice; the demons are on their way to the Royal City right now, hidden in barrels for the harvest festival. They plan to attack the city from within. If we don't confront them before they reach the gates, no one will have a chance.'

She gasped. 'I never expected they would try something like that. But Ramble, even if I do manage to raise an army, how are we going to get there in time?'

'Dragons,' he replied, hearing her inhale sharply. 'I made a deal with the rock dragons in return for rescuing one of their clan. I've asked them to meet with you, so be on the lookout. They're a big clan, and can easily carry a number of people on their backs.'

'And you're sure they're alright with that?' she said. 'I've heard that the rock dragons are a proud clan. I wouldn't want to offend them.'

'Don't worry about that; they know the situation and how much all of Treeshallow will be affected if we fail. All I need you to do is gather as many warriors, heroes, witches, wizards and mages as you can find. It will take the demons at least another five days to reach the Royal City; they can't travel any faster under that disguise. I want everyone to be ready at the city's main gates by then. I can't let the demons get inside the city, even if I manage to evacuate everyone,' he explained, realising what a crazy idea it was to try and get an army ready in less than a week.

'This is a big task,' she said heavily, 'but I won't let you down. Treeshallow won't fall to the Desrai. I'll contact you when I've gathered enough people.'

'Thank you, Wilhelmina, I don't think there's anyone else I'd trust to do this. Good luck!'

He took his staff away from his forehead and rubbed his tired eyes. Mr Rogers and Lord Tummet were looking at him with troubled expressions on their faces. 'Are you really planning to fight the demons again?' Lord Tummet asked him nervously, as though he wasn't sure if he needed permission to speak.

'Yes,' Ramble said, more sourly than he intended. 'If you hadn't helped them curse the king, then he would have found out what was going on much sooner and stopped it before it got out of hand. Though I suppose I should thank you for telling us about what the demons are up to. Things might be a lot worse if you hadn't have spoken up.'

'What do you plan on doing once we reach the city? Hogwash is confident we can reach it well before the demons get there if we ask Lightfoot and Swiftwind to push themselves again,' Hokum said, turning to face him as Small wriggled under her dangling feet.

Ramble sighed. 'I don't like to do it, but given the situation, I don't think we have much choice,' he said, leaning out the window to peer at the two unicorns pulling the carriage swiftly along the road. They saw him looking and gave a snort, bowing their heads down in a curt nod. Hogwash saw him too and gave a jaunty salute as they picked up even more speed.

'Well, that settles that,' Ramble said, pulling his head back just in time to avoid an overgrown bush. 'Once we arrive at the city, I'll alert the king and ask him to issue a warning to everyone. If we have enough time, I want the city evacuated and the people a good few miles away before any fighting starts.'

'But won't the demons see us if we pass them on the road?' Mr Rogers said after a moment.

Ramble put a hand to his chin, wondering why the thought hadn't occurred to them before, but it was Lord Tummet who answered him. 'No, they didn't come this way,' he said. 'The merchants whose barrels they're hiding in came from the south, not near here. They shouldn't have any idea what we're doing.'

'Are you absolutely sure about that?' Ramble asked him.

'I'm certain, I'm the one who ordered the barrels to be delivered to the city,' Lord Tummet replied. 'The town the merchants came from is the next one up from the one near the Door Between Worlds. The demons used the wardrobes to get there and then snuck into the barrels as the merchants passed by the field.'

Everyone looked at him with murderous stares, but Ramble shook his head at them. Terrible as it was, Lord Tummet had only helped the demons because he had been afraid, and, as he had seen from the king when he'd ran from the previous battle, fear could make people do the most idiotic of things.

24
DEFENDING THE CITY

The next few days went by very slowly for everyone in the carriage, despite Lightfoot and Swiftwind galloping along the road as fast as they could. They all knew that the longer they took to get to the Royal City, the closer to it the demons would be and the less time they would have to evacuate everyone.

As Hogwash finally pulled up to the city's golden gates on the evening of the fourth day, Ramble looked down at his hands and saw that he'd chewed every one of his finger nails in his anxiety. He hadn't heard from Wilhelmina since he'd spoken to her about the army, and the time they had before the demons arrived was only an estimate. 'You shouldn't panic so much,' Mr Rogers said. 'Panic only leads to mistakes. Besides, this plan of yours is so downright mad that it might just work.' He clapped Ramble hard on the shoulder and gave him a grin. 'It's not so very far off something that I would have done.'

Ramble simply stared at him, unsure whether he was supposed to be comforted by this.

The night guards outside the city opened the gates for them, and as they went through, he leant out of the window and told them that they'd be given orders from the king very soon. They looked surprised, but received the information seriously and took up their posts again, much more wary than before.

Hogwash steered the unicorns directly to the palace, but Ramble told him to stop around the side by the door that Princess Hurella had taken him through. 'Stay here until I come back,' he told them. 'I won't be long, but you should be able to rest Lightfoot and Swiftwind and give them some food and water. You should eat, too. I don't know if we'll get a chance to after this.'

He dashed off through the door, weaving around the chefs in the kitchens, and then entered the serving room with the dumbwaiter. He saw it sitting open, and after pushing a trolley full of cakes out of the way, he got in it and used the rope to shimmy it up towards the top floor, which he hoped was Princess Hurella's bedroom. He knew that it was impolite to enter a lady's room without her permission but, given the circumstances, he thought that she would understand.

The dumbwaiter was small and his legs started to cramp after a few seconds, but he reached the top of the shaft quickly. The serving door at the top was shut tightly, but he kicked it open with a bang.

The first thing he saw was Princess Hurella jump up from her desk with a gasp and snatch a poker from the fireplace. She stood brandishing it like a sword as he climbed out awkwardly and fell on the floor, holding his hands in the air so that she wouldn't strike him.

'Wizard Ramble?' she enquired, shocked, as his face caught the firelight. She lowered the poker and offered a hand to help him up. 'What are you doing here?'

'I'm afraid I don't have any time to explain. Please, I need you to take me to your father,' he said, standing up.

'This way,' she said, noting the urgency in his voice, and put a dressing gown over her nightdress before leading him out of the door and down the corridors to the large tapestry. Finding the right spot, she lifted it up and tapped the wall underneath. Like last time, they heard a grinding sound and the wall behind them opened up to reveal the passage behind it. They went through and found the door leading into the king's closet, turning the handle and opening it. The doors of the closet were closed, but the princess slid them open without hesitation.

'Hurella, what are you doing in here? It's late; you should be in bed,' the king said, starting in surprise and dropping the book he'd been reading. He was propped up with pillows in his enormous bed, wearing what looked like a bright flowery dressing gown.

Ramble stepped out into the room behind her, eyeing the dressing gown with amusement. The king saw him stare and lifted his blankets up so that the flowery pattern was hidden from view.

'Now, Wizard Ramble, I know I owe you for ridding me of that dreadful curse, but really! Calling at this hour, and entering through my closet no less! What's this all about?'

'Forgive me, Your Majesty,' Ramble said, remembering his manners and bowing down low, 'but you must take action immediately. The Desrai are on their way to the city, hidden in barrels being brought by merchants for the harvest festival. They shouldn't reach here until tomorrow, but we must evacuate the city well before that.'

The king stared at him, open mouthed.

'Your Majesty?' Ramble said, unsure whether the king had heard him.

King Albrand shook himself. 'How much time do we have, exactly?' he demanded, throwing back the covers and rushing over to his closet, ignoring the fact that his flowery dressing gown was on show again.

'I'm not sure. Your nephew, Lord Tummet, told us of their plans. He's waiting outside in my carriage, if you wish to question him,' Ramble replied.

The king shook his head, though appeared disturbed at the information. 'If what you're saying is true, then we need to act first and question later. I'm not going to sit here and hide like last time,' he said, tearing a set of robes from one of the hangers and throwing them on over his dressing gown. 'Hurella, please go and fetch the head guard,' he said, now pulling on a pair of trousers.

'And I think I'll fetch my maids, too,' she said, nodding.

'Maids?' the king said incredulously. 'What can they do?'

'You'd be amazed at how quickly they can spread information when they want to,' she said, before dashing from the room.

The king passed a hand over his face, and then turned to Ramble. 'I suppose you already have some sort of plan in place?' he asked, sounding hopeful.

'Yes, Your Majesty. There is an army gathering in the town near the Door Between Worlds. They should be arriving here by dragon no later than tomorrow morning,' he replied, hoping it was true.

'By dragon?' the king asked, startled, but then shook his head again. 'I'll take your word for it. Who's in this army of yours?'

'I'm...not sure yet, Your Majesty. But I know there will be plenty of strong warriors and people with magic.'

The king narrowed his eyes. 'It's unusual for you to be so disorganised,' he said, unable to keep the doubt from his voice.

'I was caught off guard. I had no idea that the Desrai would start to move yet. This is the best I can come up with.'

'I suppose it's not your fault,' the king said, and then looked at Ramble seriously. 'We can beat them again...can't we?'

'I don't know, Your Majesty. I don't even know the true size of their army, and Lord Tummet has advised me that they've come up with ways to protect themselves from fire. But I promise you, in the name of Treeshallow, that I and everyone else will do everything we can to beat them.'

The main doors to the king's bedroom opened and the head guard came in, followed by Princess Hurella and a handful of wary maids. 'Ah, finally,' the king said. 'I'll get straight to the point, Guardsman. I need you and your men, as well as all the Kingsmen you can find, to organise an evacuation of the city.'

'Sire?' the guard asked, taken aback by such a command.

'Get every man, woman and child out of the city and take them to the villages east of here. I need you to act swiftly and calmly, and if anyone starts a panic, then you must control them. Can you do this?'

'Certainly, sire,' the guard said. 'If I may, what is the reason for this?'

'The Desrai are back and heading right for us. I can't let the people get involved. I need them safe,' the king said, and then turned to the maids. 'Ladies, my daughter tells me that you are skilled at spreading information. Please help the guards and the Kingsmen as much as you can. That is all.'

The maids looked startled, but curtsied and left the room swiftly with the head guard. As the doors shut behind them, a voice sounded in Ramble's ears, one that was more welcome than anyone else's at that moment.

'Wilhelmina!' he gasped, sweeping the stick out of his robes and turning it into his staff. He placed it against his forehead, making their connection stronger.

'They're ready, Ramble,' she said, breathing heavily. 'I've got nearly a thousand, all with either exceptional fighting skills or magic...as well as a few surprises. The rock dragons are carrying us to the Royal City now.'

Ramble let out a long breath, relief spreading through his body. 'Thank you, Wilhelmina. Thank you!' he said. 'His Majesty has just ordered the city to be evacuated. I need to stay and help them for a while, but as soon as the sun rises, I'll be ready outside the city walls to meet you.'

25

THE DESRAI ARRIVE

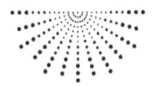

The sun began to rise, spreading its rays across the city walls and spilling over into the streets. Ramble was sitting, exhausted, on an upturned bucket in front of the main gates, having just helped the guards arrange all the carriages in the city outside the east gate so that everyone being evacuated could climb straight in and drive off.

At least, that had been the plan. As it turned out, there were several hundred more people than the carriages could take, so the king had to hold a game of picking straws to see who got the carriages and who would walk. Children were put in the carriages straight away, as the king hadn't thought it fair to make them walk when some of them could barely crawl. The adults, most of them with children themselves, had readily agreed to this, but the drawing of straws had still led to more arguments than Ramble had thought possible.

There were lords arguing with builders and seamstresses, saying that they were more valued in society and therefore had more right to a carriage than anyone else. Merchants were arguing with shopkeepers, telling them that without their bravery to travel across every part of Treeshallow for rare and valuable items, their shops would be empty, giving the merchants more right to ride in the carriages.

Teachers argued with scholars, librarians with bookbinders, and perhaps most bizarrely of all, the dinner chefs argued with the dessert chefs over whose food the king most preferred, granting them the right to a carriage.

In the end, he felt so harassed and annoyed that he used his magic to create a giant sleigh big enough to carry them all, and found two dozen rats to turn into horses to pull it.

He hadn't wanted to do it because he had been trying to conserve his magic for the battle, but he soon found that it was worth it. The second the people realised what he'd done, they all fell silent and climbed in. Some even volunteered to take the reins, and after they had sorted out the fine details, both the carriages and the sleigh pulled away and started their journey towards the eastern villages, where they would hopefully be safe.

Now the Royal City was almost empty. The people with magic had stayed at Ramble's request (though not without some complaint), as well as the guards to protect the king and Princess Hurella, who had both been adamant about staying. Mr Rogers, Lord Tummet, Hogwash and Hokum also remained to help Ramble with his strategies and for moral support.

Ramble shifted on his bucket, hearing his spine click from hunching too much. The streets behind him were silent, seeping an unusual eeriness that had replaced the usual noises of people getting ready for the day; bakers starting on their first loaves of bread and shops preparing to open.

Still, Ramble couldn't think about that now. All he could focus on was watching the sky, hoping to see the rock dragons appear on the horizon carrying the army that Wilhelmina had organised. What he didn't hope to see, however, was the merchants carrying the barrels where the demons were hiding. The thought of them turning up before his army arrived was enough to make his palms wet with sweat.

'Would you like some tea?' Princess Hurella said behind him, startling him out of his despairing thoughts.

He turned around and saw that she was holding a tray with cups and a teapot on it. He could smell the strong aroma coming from it; somewhere between flowers and soot. He pulled a face, and she laughed at him. 'It's a special blend called brew-up. I know it smells strange, but it's actually quite nice. It'll help calm you down,' she said, kneeling next to him and pouring a cup.

'I don't need calming down. I'm perfectly calm,' he protested, but his voice came out strained and ragged. 'Oh, fine,' he said, taking the cup from her and drinking a small sip.

It wasn't as bad as he expected, and was actually slightly sweet. It was much better than the Earl Grey his mother always served at home, but not quite as nice as the berry tea his father had given him once when he had helped out in his bookshop.

'See?' she said, unable to conceal her grin. She glanced up at the sky, seeing the sun rising higher to float among the clouds. 'They *will* get here in time, won't they?'

'I hope so. If they don't, then I can't promise I can hold the city by myself,' he said, drinking more tea to control the sudden shiver that had come over him.

She passed a hand through her hair and stood up, preparing to go back inside the city, but numerous black dots had appeared amid the clouds. They looked like birds at first, but they were flying so straight that she knew they couldn't be. 'Ramble, look up!' she said, balancing the tray in one hand and pointing at them with the other.

Ramble's head shot up, and his mouth broke into a wide grin. The black dots were bigger now, far too big to be any sort of bird. They were stocky and had great wings that were beating with enough power to make the clouds part slightly beside them. It was the rock dragons, and as they came close still, he could see the people riding on their backs.

But before he could celebrate, they heard a loud rumbling, like hundreds of heavy wagons coming their way. He got up, squinting into the distance, and cursed so loudly that several birds took flight. Princess Hurella's cheeks went pink, but when she followed his gaze, she said a few words that he would never have thought a princess would know. Like him, she had seen the large wagons loaded with barrels coming through the trees.

'What are we going to do?' she asked, shaking his arm in panic.

He peered up at the dragons and then back at the wagons. He couldn't tell who would get there first; it would be seconds either way. However, there was one thing he could do.

Whipping out his staff, he gripped it tightly with both hands and lifted it high into the air. The runes carved along it glowed and moved about on its surface. He concentrated on the merchants, hardly able to make out their faces from this distance. 'Fly,' he said, his voice clear and strong.

At his word, every merchant was lifted high into the air and then flew straight towards him. As they got close, Ramble stood aside and let them zoom into the city through the open gates behind him, landing neatly in a heap.

One of the merchants, whose landing hadn't been quite so hard as the others, stood up with a groan and shouted at him. 'What in Treeshallow are you doing, man?' he cried. 'Can't you see we're bringing barrels of food in for the festival? What kind of treatment is—'

The merchant's eyes widened as he looked over to the wagons. The barrels were exploding, sending great showers of splinters into the air, and out of them came the demons; thousands of them. They were tall, muscled creatures with crimson skin streaked with silver scars. Their teeth, bared in ferocious snarls, glinted gold in the sunlight, and each one was covered in dense chain mail.

They spotted Ramble outside the gates, and in one big mass, charged at the city. Steam filled the air surrounding them as they let out angry howls that made the hairs on his arms stand up as though he'd been electrocuted.

'Get back!' he yelled at Princess Hurella. 'Tell the people with magic to get here immediately and help me put up a barrier. Go!'

Princess Hurella didn't argue. She ran off into the city without looking back, leaving Ramble to face the Desrai alone. Before he could act, however, the rock dragons reached the city, roaring and swooping down to spit fire at Muldred's command. The fire licked at the demons, setting them all alight. They stopped their advance instantly, some falling to their knees and others brushing furiously at their skin, but all let out terrible, agonised shrieks.

The dragons landed in front of them, breathing yet more flames, and the people on their backs dismounted quickly and took out their weapons, wands and staffs, facing the demons with determination. Wilhelmina ran up to Ramble, just as the wizards and witches from the city, along with Hogwash, Hokum and Small, ran out of the gates and stopped dead as they saw the sight before them.

'I'm sorry we're late,' Wilhelmina said, clutching her own wand tightly. 'But everyone's ready. Give the orders and we'll fight.'

'Okay, then,' Ramble said, trying to decide quickly what to do. He inspected the people gathered there, picking out those with magic first, and then the warriors. He could see Brett and Brogar and the Dwarves of Neves, brandishing axes that looked far too big for them, and many others he recognised both from his memories and the stories he'd read on The Outside. Even the Great Caring Giant was there, towering over everyone and holding large boulders, ready to throw at the demons. What he hadn't expected to see were the goblins, and with them were creatures so similar to the demons that they could only be the Underons.

The strange sight of humans, dragons, goblins, Underons, and many others all together facing the Desrai filled him with more hope than he'd felt for a long time. The people of Treeshallow had truly come together to fight as one.

26
SWORDS AND THORNS

'Witches, wizards and mages!' Ramble called, using his magic to project his voice. 'Please come to the back line. I need you all to put up the strongest barriers you can for the warriors out on the front line. Make sure that no arrows can get through,' he said, watching the fire covering the demons fizzle out.

They were beginning to regroup, their burnt skin healing over to leave only a few chars. So *that* was what Lord Tummet had meant – they'd found a way to regenerate after being attacked with fire.

Now that they were facing an army themselves, the demons weren't so hasty to charge straight forwards. Instead, they drew out thick, jagged swords and longbows, positioning themselves so that the archers were at the back and the swordsmen were at the front.

Ramble tried hard not to dwell on the fact that their army was considerably bigger than his own, but he took comfort knowing that the demons only had normal weapons. If he organised his magic users well, then they would overthrow even the mightiest of warriors. Unfortunately, most of the people with magic in his army were healers and potion makers; hardly any of them had a background in offensive and defensive magic.

They ran to the back line as he'd directed and put up their barriers, which looked like golden panes of glass running from the ground up to sixty feet in the air. Ramble tested them individually by throwing small rocks at them, very aware that the demons were nearly ready to attack. Most of the barriers were fine, but there were three, including Wilhelmina's, that wavered dangerously every time the wind blew, revealing the lack of power in them.

'But that's all we can do,' Wilhelmina told him, trying to pour more magic into her own one. It flickered slightly, but then rippled and broke completely.

'It's alright,' he said, eyeing the row of barriers, making sure the rest all fitted together without any gaps. 'I'll expand mine to cover this area, and Hogwash and Hokum can help the other two who are struggling. What do you normally use your magic for?'

'Making tonics and potions, usually,' she said, unsure why he'd asked her something like that in such an urgent situation. 'Though I do sometimes use it to make plants grow.'

At this, his eyes lit up. 'There's a flower shop a short way into the city,' he said quickly. 'They've got some strange plants in there; one of them is an extra thorny rosebush. It's big, so get the guards to help you bring it out – they should be waiting a few streets away in case I need them.'

Wilhelmina looked at him as though he had gone mad, but did as he said and dashed off through the city gates to find the flower shop.

Ramble turned back to his army and extended his own barrier. Hogwash and Hokum, who'd been listening to the conversation, hurried over to the witch and mage who were having trouble, adding their own magic. It gave the two barriers an enormous boost, and soon they were strong enough to merge with the others so that a single, shimmering wall was formed which the warriors could retreat behind if the demons loosed their arrows.

The tension between the armies was so high that Ramble hardly dared to breathe, but as they stood facing each other, a single demon raised his bow and released an arrow with a twang that rippled through the air. As if in slow motion, Ramble watched it hit the barrier and shatter, leaving the warriors behind it unharmed.

In that instant the demons charged again, straight for the front line of Ramble's army. The warriors ran forwards to meet them, and then the air was filled with the clang of thousands of swords and shields being swung at each other with great force.

The demon archers released their arrows, but the warriors quickly jumped back behind the barrier, watching as the arrows shattered just as the first one had. The demons howled, but the warriors rushed forwards and engaged them in battle, before the next wave of arrows rained down and they retreated behind the barrier once again.

This happened another six times, and each time the demons grew angrier, and the angrier they were, the more the swings of their swords fell short. Seeing their advantage, the warriors easily ran them through.

It was messy and almost too sickening for Ramble and everyone on the back line to watch, but they held their sections of the barrier firmly. The dragons joined in with the fight too, not with fire (at Ramble's warning), but with great gusts of air from the beating of their wings. The air knocked the demons back, giving the warriors chance to adjust their grips on their weapons and wipe the blood and sweat from their brows. Even Small was contributing, despite the holes in his wings, roaring and howling along with the others.

The Great Caring Giant threw boulder upon boulder at the demons, aiming them at the archers. His height meant that his throws were accurate, and he had taken down nearly a quarter of them by the time Wilhelmina returned to Ramble's side with the great, thorny rosebush.

The guards who had helped her carry it were out of breath, but they inhaled sharply as they saw the battle, each one going paler than milk. 'You don't, er, need us here now, do you?' one of them asked.

Ramble managed to spare him a smirk. 'No, go back to the king and the princess. Keep them safe,' he said.

The guard let out a loud sigh and hurried back into the city, with the others closely behind him. 'I always thought the guards of the Royal City were fearless,' Wilhelmina mused.

Ramble shook his head. 'They're only human. Even if they were here when the last battle took place, it was very different. Back then, we knew weeks in advance about the demons' intentions, not a few days. No one was prepared for this.'

'That's true,' she replied, glancing at the battlefield and then quickly back again as she watched Brett and Brogar impale two demons directly in line with her. 'Are you going to tell me why we need this rosebush now?'

'Yes,' Ramble said. 'I want you to grow it so that it's big enough to wrap around the demons.'

'All of them? You do realise that there are still thousands of them out there, don't you?'

'Of course I do, that's exactly why I want you to do this. If the battle continues how it is, then our warriors will get tired and then they'll be the ones clumsily swinging their swords. If that happens, we'll be overrun in minutes.'

'Alright,' she said, brushing back her purple hair, which had fallen about her face. 'But it will take a long time. I can perhaps manage it in two hours, but no less than that.'

'I'll help you,' he said quickly, calculating how long the warriors could hold out. They were doing well, no one had been killed yet, though there were plenty wounded and they had no reinforcements. The demons, however, had lost several hundred, but still fought with as much vigour as when they'd started. Two hours was far too long a wait; they only had another hour at most.

'But you need to stay here and keep up your sections of the barrier,' she pointed out.

He grinned at her. 'There are *some* perks to being the most powerful wizard in Treeshallow, you know,' he said, and tapped his staff on the floor. The air around him shimmered, and when he stepped aside, she saw a perfect copy of him standing behind the barrier, still teaming with magic. 'That'll keep the barrier safe,' he said. 'Now, we've got to move this rosebush further away where the demons can't see.'

He gripped one side of the pot and she gripped the other, and together they heaved it off to the side, out of view from the main forces. 'Here should do,' he said as they reached an area just outside of the wall of barriers.

'Is it safe enough here?' Wilhelmina asked, hearing the cries from the battle all too clearly.

'If our main forces keep them occupied, then yes,' he answered, not wishing to think about what would happen if they couldn't. 'Now, if you start the spell, I'll boost it with my magic.'

'Here it goes,' she said, touching the rosebush with her bare fingers. She allowed the thorns to prick her skin a few times, before withdrawing them and holding her hands above it. The blood from her fingers dripped onto it, spattering the leaves and petals with red splotches.

Once the bleeding had stopped, she took out her wand and touched the roots, which were exposed slightly above the soil in the pot. Slowly, the rosebush began to twitch, and the blood on the leaves and petals was absorbed into it, vanishing as though it had never been there.

'It's started,' she said, indicating the stems as they slowly extended upwards. 'If you join in now, then the growth will speed up. You'll have to prick your fingers like I did first, though.'

He did as she said, letting out a wince as the thorns poked through into his skin, blushing as he remembered that she hadn't even made a sound when she'd done it. Then he let his hands bleed on the bush, splashing it with red once again. She smiled at him encouragingly, and he touched the roots with his staff.

Immediately, he felt as if his body were being stretched upwards, but after a moment he realised that he was feeling what was happening to the plant, not himself. As he got used to it, he began to pour more magic into it and watched as the plant grew to the size of a house in minutes. Maybe it would work in time.

27

RAMBLE'S MAGIC

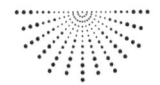

The midday sun was obscured from view as the rosebush, now so large that it was looming over the city, continued growing taller and wider. The pot it had been in had long since broken, and now the roots expanded across the ground, sinking deep into the soil.

The battle was still raging, but Ramble knew that the rosebush was almost at the size he needed it. 'Just another minute,' he said to Wilhelmina, who was shaking with the effort. He also felt the effects of using so much magic; not only from helping to grow the rosebush and maintaining his part of the barrier, but also what he'd used to help evacuate the city.

'That's it!' he cried, as the stem finally reached the low clouds drifting across the sky. Exhausted, they both fell to their knees, breathing deeply.

'How do you plan to wrap it around the demons?' she asked, looking up at it. It was so enormous that it hurt her neck trying to see the top.

'If I'm right, then I can use my magic to make the stems move about like tentacles,' he said. 'Though I think I need to catch my breath first.'

'What do you mean, if you're right?' she panted. 'You've done this type of magic before, haven't you?'

'Not exactly,' he said, avoiding her gaze. 'I read about it in a book from The Outside.'

'Oh, that's very helpful,' she said sarcastically. 'You know that the authors on The Outside always get the details wrong. How can you rely on that?'

'I'm not,' he said, managing to heave himself up using his staff. 'That's what gave me the idea. I've got my own method for making it work, though.'

She raised an eyebrow in suspicion. 'If you're confident that you can do it, then I suppose I should trust you.'

He flashed her a thumbs up and told her to wait there. With effort, he ran back to the battle to find Hogwash and Hokum.

They were still helping the witch and the mage maintain their sections of the barrier, though they too were looking strained. He opened his mouth to talk to them, but caught sight of Princess Hurella with Lightfoot and Swiftwind, kneeling by a collection of injured warriors. The unicorns were using their horns to stop the bleeding, while she tied bandages around the ones that they had already seen to.

'Princess, what are you doing here?' he asked in disbelief. 'You should be safe in the city, not here.'

'Nonsense,' she retorted defiantly. 'If I can be of use here, then here I shall stay. The barriers are enough to keep me safe.' She gave him such a stare that it left no room for argument. Cursing, he stalked back to Hogwash and Hokum.

'I knew you'd tell her off,' Hogwash said, having overheard them. 'I did tell her, but she refused to listen.'

'Well, I agree with her,' Hokum said, smiling at the princess over her shoulder. 'I wouldn't want to be drifting about behind the city walls when people could be dying outside. She's a smart woman. If she hadn't come to help, then some of our best warriors would be out of action by now.'

'Anyway,' Hogwash cut in. 'What have you and Wilhelmina been up to all the way over there? Either I'm seeing things, or there's some kind of giant bush growing there.'

'That's what I came back to tell you,' Ramble said, shaking his thoughts back together. 'I'm going to need all our warriors to pull back so that I can make the stems wrap around the demons and trap them. I'll be on the back of one of the dragons. As soon as you see me take off, give the order.'

'That's a dangerous plan,' Hogwash said. 'But then you did always like to take risks. Alright, we'll give the order when we see you.'

Ramble thanked his friends and then dashed off to speak with Muldred and Ilmar, who were in the middle of the great row of dragons, just inside the barrier. As they lowered their wings from beating another gust of air, he ran up beside them. They both blew out great rings of smoke in surprise, but once they realised it was him, they lowered their heads in greeting.

'I'm sorry to ask this of you, but I need to ride on the back of one of your clan. Can you spare someone? It's vital if we want to win this battle,' he said, hoping that they would agree.

Muldred cocked her head at him and then grumbled something to Ilmar. Ilmar grunted back to her and turned to the dragon beside him. The dragon came forwards, and with surprise Ramble realised that it was the one he'd rescued. The wing he had fixed with the leather from Mr Roger's sporran was still firmly in place, and the dragon gave a toothy grin as he saw him looking.

He lowered his neck so that Ramble could climb on his scaly back. It was awkward and more than a little uncomfortable, but Ramble managed to find a position where he felt least likely to fall off. The dragon turned to look at him, waiting for instructions.

'I need you to carry me over to that giant rosebush over there, and then back over the battlefield above the demons. Don't worry, it'll make sense when we do it,' he added, sensing the dragon's unrest. 'When you're ready.'

The dragon gave a swift nod, and beat his wings furiously into the ground, sending them soaring up into the sky. He flew over to the rosebush as Ramble had asked, and hovered in the air while the wizard took out his staff. 'Writhe,' Ramble commanded, and the stems pulsed, wriggling like snakes. In the distance, he spotted the warriors retreating from the battlefield at Hogwash and Hokum's instruction. If he was going to do it, it had to be now.

He motioned for the dragon to fly back over to the battlefield, holding his staff aloft so that the stems of the rosebush would follow him, trailing along the ground. He saw the demons trying to retreat away from the huge thorns speeding towards them, but he was too quick. In less than a minute, the rosebush had cut the demons off from his army, and now he circled his staff so that the stems spread all the way around, trapping the demons inside a dome of thorns.

A great cheer sounded from below, but Ramble knew the battle wasn't over yet. In a few minutes, the demons would cut through the rosebush. Most of them would be injured, but there would be enough to put up a fight against his tired army.

He was about to cast the spell that had defeated them last time; a great wall of flames that showered out burning arrows; but caught himself as the image of the demons' burns healing up flashed into his mind. Fire no longer worked; there had to be something else.

He gazed at the clouds rolling in from the south, trying to clear his mind, and noticed that they were dark and heavy with rain. Rain was water, and water could be frozen. He could trap the demons in ice!

The clouds burst open without him even having to use his magic, soaking him and everyone else in the area. The dome of thorns was soaked as well. Concentrating his magic on it, he enticed the sodden stems to freeze. He heard the cracking as the water took solid form, transforming the dome into a block of ice.

With a weary sigh, he asked the dragon to take him down to the ground. The dragon obliged, and once they landed, Ramble slid off his back and fell to the floor, staring up at the rain cascading down on his face. Small, who had watched them land, bounded up and licked the wizard's cheeks. The rock dragons let out a noise like a snigger as they looked on, and then, in complete unison, they let a bout of flame into the air to signal their victory.

As everyone took in what had happened, cheers erupted everywhere, and a great clatter echoed around him as humans, goblins, Underons and the Great Caring Giant let their weapons fall to the ground. Hogwash and Hokum, followed closely by Princess Hurella and the unicorns, ran over to Ramble and Small.

'Your ridiculous plan actually worked,' Hogwash said, clapping Ramble on the shoulder as Princess Hurella brought Lightfoot and Swiftwind close so that they could restore his energy.

Ramble laughed, more with relief than anything else. 'It did,' he said. 'We've beaten the Desrai outright, and there's little danger of them coming back this time.'

'And you recued Mr Rogers and your rock dragon friend. You've done everything you came back to Treeshallow for,' Hokum said softly.

He blinked at her, realising what she meant. His work was done; he could go home to The Outside and see his parents again. But that meant leaving Treeshallow. Leaving his friends.

'You can always come back again,' she added, as if reading his mind. 'The Door Between Worlds is always open to you. You can pass though it freely.'

'You're leaving Treeshallow?' Princess Hurella asked him, catching on to the conversation. 'Why?'

Before he could answer, Wilhelmina came up to them and slumped on the floor beside him. Lightfoot turned to her and began to restore her strength while Swiftwind continued healing Ramble. She patted the unicorn's neck, and then turned to the princess. 'It's a very long story, Your Highness,' she said, 'but perhaps the best explanation right now is that Wizard Ramble has family on The Outside.'

'So you're going back to see them?' the princess asked, turning to him.

Ramble eased himself up into a sitting position. 'I'll come back,' he said. 'I promise. And I won't stay away for so long this time.'

'Well, that's settled then. You will stay for the celebration feast, though, won't you?'

His stomach rumbled loudly as she spoke, and they all laughed. 'I think I will,' he said.

28

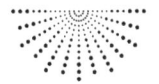

RETURN

The rock dragons stayed with them for the rest of the day and helped Ramble do the unpleasant task of piling up the demon's bodies once they had been unfrozen. They also stacked up the ones who had died by sword, and when the battlefield was finally cleared, Muldred and Ilmar breathed hot flames over the lifeless mound.

Ramble stood and watched them burn; the flames taking to the demons' bodies easily now that their fire resistant magic had dispersed with their life force. He felt no anger; he mourned. It had been exciting to read about battles, and even to remember them to an extent, but living one was very different. There was no glory in being the hero; not when so much blood had been spilt to achieve it. He wished he knew why the demons had hated the other creatures of Treeshallow so much. Perhaps if he'd known, he would have been able to come up with some sort of pact between them, but even after speaking to the Underons, who stood beside him in vigil for their fallen cousins, he had no answer. They were as baffled as he was, their lack of bloodthirst the very reason they were exiled in the first place.

The only positive thing he took from the battle was that Treeshallow was finally safe again. It was this that allowed him to enjoy the enormous feast that the king put on the next day, after everyone who had been evacuated had returned. It lasted for two whole days, due to the king's insistence that Ramble needed to make up for missing the feast after the previous battle. He didn't mind too much; it gave him chance to thank everyone for coming to his aid.

'Twas' all fer Treeshalla,' Brett and Brogar slurred, spilling their mugs of sweet wine on the palace's polished marble floor. They had been drinking heavily together since King Albrand announced the battle officially won, and were now so drunk that walking in a straight line was utterly impossible for them.

Ramble watched them wander off, sniggering as he caught then bumping into several of the sculptures lining the palace halls and apologising to each of them.

'Are you leaving today?' Wilhelmina asked, spotting him alone at the back of the banquet hall.

'Yes. Hogwash is going to take Mr Rogers and me back in the carriage, and Hokum and Small are coming along so they can see us off at the Door Between Worlds,' he replied. 'How are you getting back?'

'The Rock Dragon Clan have offered to take us,' she said. 'They're not so bad, actually, once you get over their size.'

'And how powerful their flames are,' he added with a shudder. She laughed and they walked off to see the others, listening to the joyful chatter all around them.

He woke up in the library. It was completely dark inside; the lights were off and the curtains had been drawn.

He yawned and sat up, peering through the gloom at the bookshelves looming around him.

The last thing he remembered was standing with Mr Rogers in front of the Door Between Worlds, which had become visible again because of his magic. Hogwash, Hokum and Small had been standing behind them, having already said their goodbyes. He had promised the Earth Elves that he would research their people in the Treeshallow library when he returned, and finally discover why they had gotten so small over the years.

Then he'd opened the door, letting Mr Rogers go through first.

'I'll see you on the other side, then,' Mr Rogers said, giving the rest a quick grin before disappearing through it. Ramble followed a moment after, and then that was it. He had woken up there in the dark.

He stood up, noticing that his nose only reached the middle of the bookshelves, and fumbled inside his robes for his staff to light the room. But he wasn't wearing robes. He was wearing his school uniform instead.

The library doors crashed open. Light flowed in, revealing his mother in the doorway. She saw him and cried out, running to hug him tightly.

Of course. Hokum had deactivated the spell suspending time. How had he forgotten?

'So Mr Rogers was right, you were in here,' she said, as he struggled to free himself from her grip. 'If we hadn't bumped into him on our way to the police station, then you could have had the whole neighbourhood out looking for you. Your father and I were worried sick when you didn't come home.'

'You're angry with me?' he asked uncertainly.

'No. I'm just relieved.' She drew away from him, looking into his eyes. 'What were you doing in here all this time? Why didn't you tell anyone where you were?'

'I...' he began, but he knew that she would never believe him even if he did explain.

'I assume he fell asleep reading,' Mr Rogers said, shuffling into the room. 'He must have come in here as soon as the bell went, after I was called away.'

Michael gaped at him, but the old man winked.

His mother rolled her eyes. 'I thought it must be something like that,' she said. 'Well, let's go home then.'

She led Michael out of the door, but he didn't want to go home yet.

'Hold on, mum,' he said, letting go of her hand. 'I've got to ask Mr Rogers something.'

Before she could answer, he dashed back into the library where Mr Rogers was waiting by the bookshelf labelled 'fantasy'.

'It was real, wasn't it?' he asked anxiously. 'I didn't just dream it?'

Mr Rogers smiled. 'See for yourself,' he said.

Michael bit his lip and went over to the wall by the bookshelf. He banged his fists against it like he had done before and waited. Then he heard the grinding of cogs. The bookshelf swung forwards and he breathed a sigh of relief. Behind it was an arched, red door with a knocker shaped like a tree.

The Door Between Worlds.

Dear reader,

We hope you enjoyed reading *The Door Between Worlds*. Please take a moment to leave a review, even if it's a short one. Your opinion is important to us.

Discover more books by Kathryn Wells at

https://www.nextchapter.pub/authors/kathryn-wells-fantasy-author

Want to know when one of our books is free or discounted for Kindle? Join the newsletter at

http://eepurl.com/bqqB3H

Best regards,

Kathryn Wells and the Next Chapter Team

ABOUT THE AUTHOR

Kathryn Wells is a pseudonym of author Kathryn Rossati, who loves writing fantasy, children's fiction and poetry.

As a child, she found her passion for the written word, and even though she had many other interests growing up, writing was always the one she would return to. Kathryn is also autistic and enjoys discussing her perspective of the world.

Her favourite authors are Diana Wynne Jones, Suzanne Collins, Jonathan Stroud, Neil Gaiman, Garth Nix and David Eddings, to name but a few.

For more information and to see her other works, please visit her website:

http://www.kathrynrossati.co.uk

OTHER BOOKS BY THE AUTHOR

Half-Wizard Thordric

- Unofficial Detective
- Accidental Archaeologist
- Unseasoned Adventurer